The Witches of Widdershins Academy

By
Sandra Forrester

BARRON'S

All inquiries should be addressed to:
Barron's Educational Series, Inc.
250 Wireless Boulevard
Hauppauge, New York 11788
http://www.barronseduc.com

Library of Congress Catalog Control Number: 2006015566

ISBN-13: 978-7641-3578-1
ISBN-10: 0-7641-3578-3

Library of Congress Cataloging-in-Publication Data

Forrester, Sandra.
  The witches of Widdershins Academy / by Sandra Forrester.
    p. cm.
  "Cover illustration and maps by Nancy Lane"—T.p. verso.
  Summary: After being classified as Classical witches, Beatrice Bailey (AKA
Bailiwick) and her friends are off to Widdershins, a witches' academy, where
they deal with the mystery of the town's monster and also make a discovery
that changes the life of one of them.
  ISBN-13: 978-0-7641-3578-1
  ISBN-10 0-7641-3578-3
  [1. Witches—Fiction.] I. Title.

PZ7.F7717Wow2007
[Fic]—dc22
                                                        2006015566
PRINTED IN THE UNITED STATES OF AMERICA
9 8 7 6 5 4 3 2 1

Contents

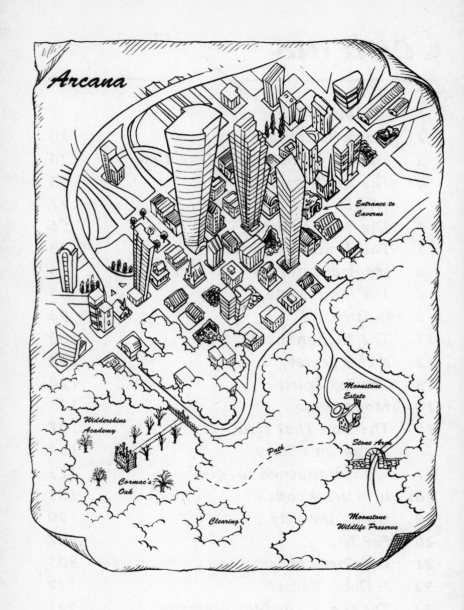

1

The Witch Examiner

Beatrice woke up that morning thinking, *Today's the day. The witch examiner will be here in*—She glanced at the clock on her bedside table and saw that it was 6:28. *In exactly one hour and . . . thirty-two minutes.*

She reached up to stroke the sleeping cat that felt like a twenty-pound bag of sand against her shoulder. "Oh, Cayenne," Beatrice said softly, "what have we gotten ourselves into?"

Snow was falling outside her window. It was unusually cold for early December, and Beatrice could hear the furnace clanking and groaning, trying hard, but not doing a very good job of heating the old house. She threw back the pile of covers and leaped out of bed, shivering as she grabbed for her robe and fuzzy, green dragon slippers.

Beatrice was tall and skinny, with pale red hair that brushed her shoulders and silky bangs that had a habit of falling into her green-gold eyes. She looked pretty much like any other eighth-grade girl, but as most of her classmates and neighbors had long suspected, Beatrice Bailey was different. After thirteen years, she had *almost* gotten used to the curious stares and whispered gossip that followed her wherever she went, but that didn't mean she liked it. Beatrice and her three best friends— Teddy Berry, Ollie Tibbs, and Cyrus Rascallion—had learned early that being a witch in the mortal world was rarely easy.

Beatrice headed for the bathroom. A hot shower soon warmed her up, but did little to wash away her anxiety. The more she thought about facing that witch examiner this morning, the closer she came to jumping back into bed and forgetting the whole thing. What if she flunked the exams? Then the Witches' Executive Committee would realize that they'd made a mistake, that they should have classified her as an Everyday witch, like her parents, instead of making her Classical—which meant they thought she was capable of working important magic. *Important magic?* Despite the fact that Beatrice was descended from the old witch family of Bailiwick, and had a long string of illustrious ancestors, she could cast only one kind of spell without goofing it up. Was *that* the mark of a Classical witch?

She had always known that her magical powers were limited, so when the Witches' Executive Committee had shown up on her twelfth birthday to announce her classification, Beatrice had been prepared to hear the word *Everyday*. Imagine her astonishment when the committee had said they were undecided about her classification, that she'd have to be tested.

Teddy, Ollie, and Cyrus had offered to help with the test, which required them to travel to the Witches' Sphere five different times and risk their lives over and over as they tried to break a diabolical spell cast by the evil sorcerer Dally Rumpe. Since her friends' magical abilities were no more impressive than her own, Beatrice had had her doubts that they'd ever be able to pull it off. But somehow—with assistance from Beatrice's cousin, Miranda Pengilly, and from other new friends they'd made along the way—the spell had finally been broken and the young witches had received their classifications. They were now Classical witches, and, as such, eligible to attend a witch academy in the Sphere where they would learn all the magical ins and outs expected of them as new members of an elite circle. But first, they had to take those entrance exams.

As Beatrice stepped out of the shower, she was giving herself a pep talk. "It's just some written tests," she muttered. "No big deal."

But Beatrice had learned the hard way that when witches from the Sphere got involved, you could never assume anything. Nasty surprises seemed to follow them around like a stubborn case of witch fever.

She was putting on jeans and a heavy sweater when Cayenne—who was long-haired and quite large, most closely resembling a black-and-orange feather duster on legs—padded into the bathroom and started yowling for her breakfast.

"Okay, okay," Beatrice said as she gave her hair a swipe with the brush. "But don't get your hopes up. You hear those pans clanging downstairs? Sounds like Mom's trying to make something from scratch."

And sure enough, when Beatrice walked into the kitchen, with Cayenne sprinting ahead, she saw that the stove and counters were covered with pots and pans. And standing in their midst was her mother, stirring something and mumbling what sounded very much like the words to a spell.

Beatrice's father was sitting at the table, calmly drinking a cup of coffee. When she gave him an inquiring look, he just rolled his eyes.

"Oh, there you are," Mrs. Bailey said when she saw Beatrice. "Just in time for breakfast."

"Um—You didn't have to go to so much trouble," Beatrice said.

"Oh, it's no trouble at all," her mother answered. "This is a big day, sweetie. You need fortification before you go into those exams."

Beatrice poured herself a glass of orange juice and sat down across from her father. Cayenne was pacing around the room, switching her tail and giving Beatrice dark looks.

"She's using magic?" Beatrice whispered.

"Well," Mr. Bailey said softly, and then he sighed. "At least nothing's blown up yet."

Beatrice's mom wasn't much of a cook under any circumstances, but when she combined cooking and magic, the results could be disastrous.

Mr. and Mrs. Bailey were both tall and skinny, and Mrs. Bailey had the same pale red hair as her daughter. Mr. Bailey didn't have much hair at all. They were both

4

wearing khaki pants and forest-green shirts with *Bailey Nursery & Garden Center* embroidered across the front.

"*Voila!*" Mrs. Bailey said with a dramatic wave of the wooden spoon she was holding. "It's ready. I hope you're both hungry. There's an awful lot of food."

And as Mrs. Bailey brought platter after platter to the table, Beatrice saw that she hadn't exaggerated. Of course, not all the food would have been identifiable if her mother hadn't said things like, "Here's the French toast, with applesauce and cinnamon," and "I know how you love anchovies and mushrooms in your omelet."

When the table was finally loaded down, and Beatrice and her father were just sitting there staring at it all, Mrs. Bailey paused to actually look at what she was serving.

"Oh, dear," she said, her eyebrows coming together in a frown. "I must have left out something. The French toast isn't quite . . . firm."

Beatrice and Mr. Bailey protested that everything looked perfect and started filling their plates like they couldn't wait to dig in. But, in truth, the French toast *wasn't* firm—Beatrice had to pour it onto her plate— and the omelet had the consistency of a wool mitten. A sausage link bent her fork, so she switched to bacon, which looked and tasted like a charcoal briquette. Cayenne sniffed with disdain at some bits of blackened bacon, then buried them under the rug. She had to resign herself to a bowl of dry cat food.

When the phone rang, Beatrice was on her feet in a nanosecond, grateful for any reason to leave the table.

"Hello, Bailey residence . . . Oh, hi, Teddy . . . Um—jeans . . . My red sweater . . . No, that sounds fine . . . Really . . . *Really*, Teddy, I don't think it matters what we wear . . . How about your black pants? . . . Okay, then your blue ones . . . Teddy, calm down . . . *Teddy!* Listen to me. You'll do fine. Just take a deep breath . . . I'll be leaving in a few minutes . . . Um—five . . . Yes. Five *exactly* . . . Bye."

Beatrice hung up and came back to the table.

Mrs. Bailey had filled her own plate and was scooping up a bite of French toast with a spoon. "Teddy's worried about the exams," she guessed.

"Freaked out is more like it," Beatrice said. And it was obviously catching because her own heart was thumping against her ribs like crazy and her stomach was turning flips. There was no way she could force down another bite of that woolly omelet, so she took a sip of juice and said, "Thanks for the wonderful breakfast, Mom."

"But you've just picked at your food," Mrs. Bailey protested.

"Nerves," Mr. Bailey said, then caught Beatrice's eye and winked.

"I'd better get over to Ollie's," Beatrice said, "before Teddy loses it completely."

"Why are they giving the exam at Ollie's?" Mr. Bailey asked. "The examiner could have come here."

"Ollie has that big schoolroom," Beatrice said as she put on her jacket. "Since he's homeschooled, he's all set up for tests, so Mrs. Tibbs offered the space."

"We know you'll do great," Mrs. Bailey told her. She sounded calm, but Beatrice could see the familiar mixture of excitement and dread in her face. Her mother wanted her to succeed. Her mother didn't want to lose her. And she couldn't have both.

"After everything you kids have been through," Mr. Bailey said, "this'll be a piece of cake, sweetheart."

"Thanks," Beatrice said. She picked up Cayenne and tucked the cat into the front of her jacket. Then she followed her own advice to Teddy and took a deep breath. "Well, wish me luck," she said.

It was snowing hard as Beatrice walked down the porch steps to the front yard. In fact, the snow was beginning to drift, and the big white house with the gingerbread trim looked like it had been created from spun sugar, an elaborate confection for a giant. Only the lime-green shutters and jewel-toned witch balls in the window were at odds with the illusion.

Beatrice started down the sidewalk and slipped. The pavement was turning icy. "I'd better take care of this," she said to Cayenne.

Then she began to mumble:

> *Circle of magic, hear my plea,*
> *Howling winds,*
> *Blowing snow,*
> *This I ask you: make them go.*

Instantly, the wind died down, the snow stopped, and the sun came out. This was the sum total of Beatrice's magical talent: She could control the weather.

She was thinking about this—brooding, actually—as she and Cayenne headed toward Ollie's house. It was pathetic, really. Here she was, a Classical witch, and all she could do was cast *weather spells?*

Before the Witches' Executive Committee had come up with that test, Beatrice had been resigned to the idea of becoming an Everyday witch. She'd never dreamed of being the greatest witch who ever lived, like Teddy. And unlike Ollie, who came from an old, revered witch family that was always pushing him to excel, Beatrice had known that her parents would have been proud of her if she hadn't been able to do any magic at all. Her cousin, Miranda, on the other hand, was ambitious—even more driven than Teddy. Miranda had been willing to do just about anything to break Dally Rumpe's spell and claim all the glory for herself, even playing dirty tricks on Beatrice and her friends that had put them all in danger. But then Miranda had turned herself around. She was still self-centered and pushy, but she'd ended up becoming a loyal friend. And Cyrus? Well, Cyrus had never seemed to care one way or the other about this Classical thing. He just wanted to have a good time.

At that particular moment, Beatrice envied Cyrus. She wished she could be more like him, taking each day as it came and not agonizing over the future. But ever since they'd broken Dally Rumpe's spell, and Beatrice had realized that she might actually stand a chance of becoming Classical, she'd started to *want* this new and different kind of life. She wanted it *bad!* And the thought of having to go back to the way she'd always lived, to watching everything she said and did, and *still* being regarded as a weirdo by the mortals in this town— Well, she didn't think she could do it anymore. She just *had* to pass those exams.

They were approaching Ollie's house, which was big and white like Beatrice's, but a little less subtle. In fact, there were things about it that just screamed, *Witch!* The stepping-stones out front, for instance, inscribed with sayings like, *Bright blessings upon you.* And *Merry meet,* and *merry part,* and *merry meet again.* And the weather vane—a witch riding on a broomstick—which caused the neighbors considerable distress.

Beatrice was passing the house next door to Ollie's when suddenly, something caught her eye. An animal was crouched under the neighbor's front steps, its fur a brilliant coppery-red. It was too big to be a cat. *Maybe a dog,* Beatrice thought. But the creature was in shadow and she couldn't really tell. Then it started to move, inching forward into the sunlight, and she saw a face that looked exactly like—*a fox.* But that didn't seem likely.

"Beatrice!"

It was Teddy, calling to her from Ollie's porch. Beatrice waved and then turned back to the animal under the steps. But it was gone! Somehow, in about two seconds, it had managed to disappear.

Beatrice scanned the snow-covered yard, her eyes lingering around the neighbor's steps. *Now this is weird,* she thought. Because the snow was perfectly smooth, without a single paw print.

"Beatrice!" Teddy called again, clearly agitated. "Hurry up! We're going to be late."

Glancing at her watch, Beatrice saw that they still had seventeen minutes, but she thought it best to humor her friend. Anything to avoid a case of full-blown hysteria.

Teddy was pacing up and down the porch when Beatrice got there. She was petite and pretty, with short brown curls and dark eyes behind oversized wire-rimmed glasses. Beatrice noticed that she'd settled on jeans, a cream-colored sweater, and her chartreuse ski jacket. She looked great—except for a certain crazed look in her eyes.

"I know you'll think I'm nuts," Teddy burst out, without bothering to say hello. "You'll just tell me it's nerves, but all the time I've been standing here waiting for you, I've had the strangest feeling. Like somebody's staring at me. I'm pretty sure I'm being watched!"

"I don't think you're nuts," Beatrice said. "You've always been able to sense these things. Do your spell and find out."

So Teddy began to chant:

> *Candle, bell, and willow tree,*
> *Who does snoop and spy on me?*
> *Use your magic for our side,*
> *Show us who would wish to hide.*

Suddenly, the metal umbrella stand beside Ollie's front door tipped over and clattered to the porch floor, revealing a tiny creature no more than three inches tall who'd been crouching behind it.

"Cyrus!" Teddy said sharply. "Why are you hiding? And why did you shrink yourself? This is no time to show off your one and only spell!"

Tilting his head back to look up at them, Cyrus said in a small voice that fit his diminutive size, "I shrunk myself because I didn't want the two of you seeing me. I knew you'd try to talk me into going inside, and I don't want to take those exams!"

"Honestly, Cyrus," Teddy muttered.

"I'm not as smart as the rest of you," Cyrus went on mournfully, "so I'll never pass. Besides, going on an adventure to the Witches' Sphere is one thing, but *living* there is something else again. And you know how much I hate witch food. If I *were* to go, I'd probably starve!"

"Cyrus, you *are* smart," Beatrice assured him, but Teddy was talking over her.

"There isn't time for you to have a meltdown," Teddy said firmly to Cyrus. "So make yourself big again. *Right this minute.*"

Cyrus sighed deeply, but then began to chant:

By the mysteries, one and all,
Make me grow from small to tall.

It was at that moment that Beatrice caught a flash of color out of the corner of her eye. She turned toward the house next door and saw that animal again—copper-coated, glowing, with a white tip on its bushy tail—dashing along the chain-link fence to the backyard. There were no bushes for it to hide behind, no way for it to escape except by going over the fence—and yet, right in front of Beatrice's eyes, the creature vanished!

She stared hard at the spot where the animal had been. Again, there were no marks in the snow. But she had seen it clearly this time. And now, at least, she was certain of one thing: It was definitely a fox.

Cyrus was finishing his counterspell.

Let me from this spell be free,
As my will, so mote it be.

As soon as he'd uttered the final word, he was his normal size again, which was still not very big. He was at least a head shorter than Beatrice.

She stood there looking at him with concern, at the wide mouth that was usually smiling, but was now pulled down at the corners, and at the brilliant blue eyes that were almost always twinkling in his small, pointed face, but were now lifeless, a clear reflection of his misery.

"Cyrus, what's going on?" she asked gently. "You're the one who's always craving new experiences and looking forward to the next adventure. I've never seen you like this."

Cyrus bowed his head, his black hair shining in the sun. "I don't know," he said softly. Then he looked up at her with a bewildered expression. "I just have this feeling that—that something really bad is going to happen if we go back to the Sphere."

Before Beatrice could respond, Teddy grabbed hold of Cyrus's arm to keep him from bolting, and said, "Well, get over it! You're taking those exams with the rest of us. And you're going to pass!"

She rang the doorbell, which sounded like the snarl of a werewolf, and the door slowly opened. No one was standing there, but they knew the drill, so they stepped inside and started taking off their scarves and jackets. A large brown owl swooped down the staircase and made a grab for their discarded clothing with his beak.

About that time, Mrs. Tibbs came to greet them. She was blond and willowy, with bare feet showing beneath a long, full skirt. Behind her, Beatrice could see a mob of people crammed into the Tibbses' living room, all of them talking and laughing and lifting their glasses in a toast.

"Come in, come in," Mrs. Tibbs said gaily, and following Beatrice's gaze, she added, "The whole family's gathered to support Oliver today. We're so thrilled about your classifications, and we just know you'll all do brilliantly on the exams. It's almost time, so why don't I take you back to the schoolroom?"

As they trooped down the long hall, Beatrice found herself thinking about the fox. How it had disappeared and then come back. Or had it just been hiding? Maybe Teddy's spell had exposed it. But how had the animal managed to vanish the second time, seemingly into thin air? And without leaving so much as one paw print behind.

Mrs. Tibbs opened the door to the schoolroom, and there was Ollie, sitting on a corner of the long library table. He was tall and thin like his mother, with green eyes and hair the color of lemon custard. He seemed preoccupied, staring out the window and tapping a quilled pen on the table. But then he turned around as he heard them come into the room and his face lit up. Beatrice thought Ollie Tibbs was the most handsome boy she had ever seen, and about the nicest, too. On that last trip to the Sphere, their relationship had changed from friendship to, well, more than friendship. Beatrice was wearing the silver bracelet he had given her, with the charm of a castle that was a replica of her ancestral home. She hadn't taken it off since Ollie had put it on her wrist the night of the victory banquet.

Now he was looking straight at her, grinning. And Beatrice was grinning back, thinking, *Here's another reason why I have to do well on these exams.* Ollie was brilliant, and even if he wasn't especially gifted in the applications of magic, he'd been studying witch history and prophecy and all that other magical stuff under his family's careful supervision for years. So he was bound to get into a good academy—and Beatrice had her heart set on being there with him.

Ollie pulled out a chair for Teddy, one for Cayenne, and then one for Beatrice beside his own.

"Did you study those books on the history of magic I gave you?" he asked as they were sitting down.

But then two things happened, and Beatrice didn't have a chance to answer.

First, her cousin Miranda came sweeping through the door wearing the most beautiful burgundy silk robes Beatrice had ever seen. Miranda was always dressed like she'd just come from a fashion shoot for *Traditional Witch*, but she usually didn't go *this* far. Not while she was in the mortal world, anyway.

Beatrice waved and Miranda gave her a dazzling smile. Teddy was undeniably pretty, but Miranda was gorgeous, which had led to plenty of tense moments between the two, since both were used to being the best-looking witch in the room. But now Miranda greeted Teddy warmly, and then Teddy said something to make Miranda laugh, so Beatrice assumed that all was well.

Miranda was even taller than Beatrice, with short dark hair and smoky-lashed gray eyes that were so pale they were almost silver. With a pointed hat perched jauntily on her head, she looked stunning.

"Not overdressed or anything, are we?" Beatrice called out to her cousin with a grin.

Miranda grinned back and answered, "Well, I thought I'd *look* the part, at least."

And that's when the second thing happened. All of a sudden the house began to quiver, then to shake with a vengeance. Gasping in surprise, everyone reached for something to hold on to and turned instinctively toward the door, just in time to see a flash of light that momentarily blinded them.

Beatrice blinked and rubbed her eyes, and when she looked again, she saw a figure standing in the doorway. It was, of course . . . the witch examiner.

Worse Than Horrible

With her skinny arms wrapped around an enormous stack of papers, the witch examiner hobbled into the room as if her corns were giving her a fit. In black robes that were frayed and faded, and a pointed black hat that listed to one side, she had a pinched face that was faintly yellow, like cookie dough, with tiny, black-currant eyes pushed into it, one higher than the other.

Those eyes flitted from face to face as she took them all in. And then, with a snort that seemed to say she wasn't impressed, she introduced herself in a raspy voice as Verna Beet, Chief of the Witch Examination Office.

Ollie's mother stepped forward to welcome her, but the witch examiner cut her off midword and said, "Get out!"

Mrs. Tibbs's jaw dropped, but she recovered quickly, squaring her shoulders and murmuring, "Why, of course. You need to get started."

After Mrs. Tibbs was gone, Verna Beet stared hard at the door and it slammed shut. Then her eyes fell on Cayenne, who slid down in her chair under the witch examiner's impaling gaze. Beatrice was chewing her lip, trying to remember if there had been anything in the exam literature about cat-familiars not being allowed in the testing room. But there must not have been because Verna Beet had already turned away from Cayenne and was dumping her papers onto the table.

"Everyone sit!" the witch examiner barked, and those who were standing skittered to chairs behind the table.

The next thing Beatrice knew, papers were flying from the pile and landing in front of her and the others, shuffling themselves into neat—and increasingly tall—stacks. Beatrice tried to keep track of the number of pages accumulating before her, but she lost count after sixty-seven.

As quill pens and bottles of ink suddenly appeared at the elbow of each witch to be tested, Verna Beet said, "These are your exams. The first set measures your knowledge in various disciplines—from the creation and use of magical defense potions to witch etiquette. The second set determines aptitude, and the third consists of a variety of psychological tests. Need I say that these exams could be the most important you'll ever take in your lives?" Then she actually chuckled, but it came out as a small, nasty explosion in the otherwise silent room.

"The rules are as follows," she went on, her eyes glinting as they slid down the row of tense faces in front of her. "No talking. No eating. No drinking. No breaks.

No glancing at your neighbor's paper. Remain in your seats until everyone is finished. All right, you may *begin*."

The exams went on for hours. They were grueling for everyone except Cayenne, who slept through them. Not that Beatrice didn't know *any* of the answers. Her parents grew herbs to sell at the garden center and she'd helped tend them and could name most of their uses. And it was to her advantage that she'd actually been to the Witches' Sphere because she'd had firsthand experience with different sorts of magic-folk, like gnomes and water leapers and spriggans. But a lot of the questions didn't ring any bells at all.

Beatrice blew her bangs out of her eyes and reread some she had skipped. She had no idea what thrummy-caps and kobolds were. Nor the proper way to greet a tantarrabob. And the name of the Fairy Queen of the Midnight Court? Could it be . . . *Rumpelstiltskin?*

Morning turned to afternoon, and then to late afternoon. Beatrice was finally ready to begin the psychological tests. They were multiple-choice, so that had to be easier, right? But the very first question stumped her.

Which of the following gifts would you most like to receive for your birthday? The choices were: *a) the fifteen-volume set of* Influences of Vampire Feeding Habits on Social Culture, *b) music by witch rocker Marley Mayhem,* or *c) a pet vulture.* There was no selection for *None of the above.*

The words started to blur in front of Beatrice's eyes. She was tired. She was hungry. She needed to go to the bathroom and maybe walk around a little to get the feeling back in her feet. But she knew the rules.

She straightened up to work a kink out of her neck and saw that her friends looked pretty awful, too. Teddy was slumped in her chair, staring at the page in front of her as if willing it to reveal the answers. Miranda was clenching, then unclenching, her fists and muttering under her breath. Cyrus was just sitting there with his head in his hands. Only Ollie was actually writing, furiously, a look of desperation on his face. And there was Verna Beet at the front of the room, picking her teeth with a quill feather.

Disgusted, Beatrice looked away and her eyes fell on the window. It was snowing again, a wet, heavy snow that stuck to bare branches and turned rooftops white. The whole world outside that room was white. Except . . . Beatrice leaned forward and stared. Except for one spot of bright color in Ollie's backyard. The fox was back.

It was perched on a snow-covered picnic table not twenty feet away, and it seemed to be—yes, it was definitely staring into the schoolroom.

The exams were finally over. Verna Beet held out her hands and the test papers flew into them. Then, with a curt, "Merry part," she disappeared.

It was dark outside. Beatrice stood up and stretched, feeling wobbly and disoriented. No one said a word. Beyond speech, they just wandered off in a daze toward the various bathrooms in the house as Mrs. Tibbs yelled after them to call their parents and say they'd be staying for dinner.

Beatrice had recovered a little by the time she and Cayenne rejoined the others. All the Tibbs relatives were gone, and Beatrice had seen Ollie's father reading the newspaper when she passed his study, so the only ones gathered in the kitchen were Mrs. Tibbs, Beatrice's friends, and Miranda. *And*—Beatrice realized with a start—Dr. Featherstone.

Beatrice had first met Aura Featherstone when the Witches' Executive Committee had appeared at her twelfth birthday party. The attractive, auburn-haired witch in emerald-green robes had stood out from her more somber—and, mostly, disinterested—colleagues. She could be intimidating, no doubt about it, but Beatrice had always found her to be supportive and caring. In fact, it was Dr. Featherstone who'd pushed for Beatrice and her friends to be tested in the first place. This was partly because Aura Featherstone and Beatrice's mother had been friends when they were young, and partly because of a hunch Dr. Featherstone had that Beatrice Bailey was destined for greater things than hanging out at the mall and learning algebra. A quaint mortal invention, algebra, and as everyone knew, totally useless.

Still, Dr. Featherstone was an important executive, with a busy schedule, and Beatrice hadn't expected to find her in the Tibbses' kitchen. But there she was, sitting at the table with Teddy, Cyrus, and Miranda, while Ollie helped his mother fix dinner.

Dr. Featherstone positively beamed at Beatrice and said, "I wanted to be here when you all finished your exams. Now that they're out of the way, the worst is over."

Probably not, Beatrice thought. The worst would come when she was notified that her Classical classification had been revoked. She was sure they could do that, and would. In fact, after her showing on those exams today, she'd be lucky if they let her be an *Everyday* witch.

"So tell me about the exams," Dr. Featherstone said, looking first at Beatrice and then the others. "Were they difficult? Easy?"

"Not easy," Ollie said, his face still pasty and a little grim.

"I'm sure I did fine," Miranda said, never one to doubt herself, at least not publicly, "but I agree with Ollie. They weren't easy."

"Oh, for pity's sake," Teddy grumbled, "just admit it, Miranda, they were horrendous."

"Well . . . ," Miranda murmured, "I wouldn't say *horrendous.*"

"You wouldn't?" Teddy shot back. "Then name the four animals mentioned in Merlin's Moldwarp Prophecy. And while you're at it, why don't you tell us what the baku eats?"

Miranda's face went tight and it was obvious that she had no clue what the answers were. But Mrs. Tibbs stepped in smoothly and said, "You're all just tired. I'm sure you did much better than you think."

"Not me," Cyrus said quietly. He had been sitting there with his chin propped up on his hands, looking defeated. "I know I flunked—especially the psychological part."

Dr. Featherstone gave him a long, searching look. "Cyrus," she said finally, "it's impossible to *flunk* the psychological tests."

Cyrus just shrugged, not appearing reassured at all.

"But even if we do pass," Ollie said, "won't it be hard starting at a witch academy midyear?"

"You won't be," Dr. Featherstone answered. "In the Witches' Sphere, the school year starts in January."

Beatrice had just been listening and not saying anything, although she agreed completely with Teddy. Those exams had been horrible, and Verna Beet had been horrible—no, *worse* than horrible—and if this was any indication of what life at a witch academy was going to be like, she was pretty sure she didn't want to go there. But Dr. Featherstone was so excited for them, Beatrice didn't have the heart to burst her bubble.

Now Teddy and Miranda were asking Dr. Featherstone about the different witch academies and where they should apply.

"Apply to any that interest you," Dr. Featherstone said. "Has anyone explained the academy system to you? No? Well, the junior academies, the ones for little witches, teach general magic and are all pretty much alike, but each of the senior academies—where you'll be going—focuses on a particular field of study. One might specialize in the healing arts, for example, another in the creation and casting of spells and counterspells. Just keep in mind that the Assignments Board at the Department of Witch Education will determine where you go. They'll take your preferences into account, but their decision is based primarily on your student file and test results."

Teddy groaned. "Then I'm dead. I'll never get into one of my top choices."

"Me, either," Ollie said. "Not if they're using those exam scores."

And that's when Dr. Featherstone's patience ran out. "So *what* if you don't get into the academy of your choice?" she demanded, hazel eyes flashing. "Just about any school in the system is first-rate in its particular field. And have you forgotten that not very long ago you weren't even eligible to attend an academy? But as Classical witches, you're assured of getting in *somewhere*. I'd call that a step up, wouldn't you?"

She's right, Beatrice thought, *we're getting greedy. Just please, please, please let me stay a Classical witch and I won't care which academy I go to. As long as it's with Ollie.*

But Teddy seemed unfazed by the witch's outburst. "Dr. Featherstone, I've been wondering," she said, "which academy did you attend?"

"Honoria Wagstaffe," Dr. Featherstone replied, and her mood changed instantly to one of fond remembrance. "Wonderful school. Their focus is on teaching witch management and leadership skills. A lot of my associates at the Institute went there."

Beatrice saw a light come on simultaneously in Teddy's and Miranda's heads. There was no question now where *they* were going to apply.

"How many years were you there?" Miranda asked.

"Three," Dr. Featherstone said, "but each witch learns at his or her own pace. You might stay for four years, or even five. And then, if you show promise for advanced study, you can go on to Witch U."

"Dinner's almost ready," Mrs. Tibbs broke in, "and I want you all to stop worrying and enjoy the food and the pleasant company. Oliver, why don't you make us some cat's purr tea? That's always soothing."

So Ollie filled a pot with water and started to chant:

> Heat of flame, heat of fire,
> Give to me my one desire.
> Boil this water, bubbling free,
> As my will, so mote it be!

And the water began to boil.

After dinner, when everyone was getting ready to leave, Ollie offered to walk Beatrice home. They put on their jackets, Beatrice tucked Cayenne into the front of hers, and she and Ollie stepped outside into the cold night. It had stopped snowing, and overhead, stars were twinkling, sharp-edged and brilliant against the black sky.

As they started down the sidewalk, Beatrice remembered the fox and looked for it, but it was either gone or hidden by the darkness. Then Ollie reached for her hand, and she forgot all about the fox. Conscious only of the warmth of his fingers intertwined with hers and her heart beating very fast, Beatrice even forgot to worry about exams and witch academies. Had they crossed her mind at all, she probably would have believed that everything was going to work out fine. Because it was nearly impossible to feel this happy and to think gloomy thoughts at the same time.

But at that exact moment, far away in the Witches' Sphere, events were unfolding that would have shaken Beatrice's optimism had she known about them. Tangled secrets that had been kept too long were about to erupt.

In a small, book-lined room, the flame of a candle flickered as a hand moved across the desk to dip a quill pen into ink. Then the hand came to rest on a piece of parchment, where it wrote the name *Beatrice Bailiwick*.

Less than a mile away, two figures stood on a dark city street, shoulders hunched against the cold.

"I don't know why you're worried," one of them said. "They're just kids."

"Kids who defeated one of the most powerful sorcerers in the Sphere," the other growled, "so they must have strong powers of their own. Especially that Bailiwick girl. She's the leader. What if she gets suspicious and starts nosing around?"

"That could be a problem."

"Not if we take care of it now. We'll just have to get rid of her."

And in a nearby field, a small, red fox trilled its ancient song to the moon and then slipped beneath the roots of a tree to its hidden den. To wait.

3

Moving in the Wrong Direction

Beatrice and Ollie were poring over one of the witch academy catalogues spread across the floor of her room, while Teddy worked on her application at the computer. Cyrus was stretched out on the rug, staring at the ceiling.

"So," Teddy said as she clicked *Print*, "have you guys decided yet?"

"Delphinius Bellows Academy," Ollie said, "named for the famous witch scholar of the seventeenth century."

Beatrice sighed. "It's a school for brains. They have more students accepted into Witch U than any other academy."

Ollie grinned. "Isn't that great?"

"For you, maybe," Beatrice shot back, "but I'm no brain."

Looking worried, Ollie said, "Don't tell me you're backing out. You *are* applying to Delphinius Bellows."

"I've already filled out the application," Beatrice said. But she didn't think she had a chance of getting in, which was why she'd asked Ollie to look at the catalogues again so they could pick a couple of backup schools.

Teddy glanced down at Cyrus, who was still sprawled on the floor with his hands behind his head. "What about you, Cyrus? Have you even opened any of the catalogues?"

"I'm applying to Mystic Isle," he said, his tone suggesting this was comparable to having a math test and an appendectomy on the same day.

"Glad to see you so excited about it," Teddy drawled. Then she said, "Mystic Isle . . . Isn't that the one with pictures of kids leaping around bonfires and riding the waves on giant sea horses? It's a play school."

Cyrus raised his shoulders in a shrug. "So what's wrong with that?"

Beatrice noticed her lit book under a stack of catalogues and said, "Don't forget, Teddy, we have that test in English tomorrow."

"Who cares?" Teddy responded.

Beatrice had thought she'd never see the day when Teddy brushed off grades. But then, why *should* they care? Their parents were making them finish out the semester—mainly, to keep up appearances—but the witch academies wouldn't give a hoot what they'd done in a mortal school. Which reminded her . . .

"I meant to tell you guys," she said, "word's out about us going away to boarding school. Amanda Bugg stopped me in the hall today and wanted to know the name of the institution. The *institution!* Like they were locking us up—and about time, too."

Teddy grinned. "Wouldn't she just die if she knew? I tell you, she's *one* mortal I won't miss. And I can name some others in this town."

Beatrice felt the same way. But she was really going to miss her parents. And this house . . . She looked around the room that had been hers for thirteen years and felt a tightness in her throat. Then she tried to imagine not seeing Teddy and Cyrus every day, but she couldn't. They'd all been friends for as long as she could remember. What was she going to do without them?

Teddy retrieved her application from the printer and said casually, "I thought Miranda might be here this afternoon."

Beatrice was thumbing through another catalogue. "It's a long drive from Henderson. Her mother didn't have time to bring her."

"Oh." Teddy sounded disappointed. "I was just going to ask her where she's applying."

Beatrice looked up at her friend and grinned. "Teddy, you *know* where Miranda's applying. Maybe you two can be roommates."

"Sure, joke about it," Teddy muttered. "But it's going to be so stressful with her there. You know how competitive she is. She has to make the best grades and have the best clothes . . . She just has to be the *best*."

Beatrice decided not to point out that Teddy had just described herself.

With applications mailed and school out for Winter Break, all Beatrice and her friends had to do now was wait for their acceptance letters. Teddy called twenty times a day to see if Beatrice had gotten hers yet, while Miranda sent an e-mail about every half hour asking the same thing. And long after the mail had been delivered, Beatrice found herself running out to the box to check again, just in case she'd overlooked it. Then, two days before Christmas, she went to the mailbox without any hope of finding the letter—and there it was! A long, cream-colored envelope addressed in black ink to *Beatrice Bailiwick, a.k.a., Beatrice Bailey.*

Her hands were shaking as she went back inside. She stood in the front hall for a full minute, clutching the envelope and trying to catch her breath, before tearing it open and pulling out the letter.

"Dear Ms. Bailiwick," she read, *"We are delighted to inform you that you have been accepted at Widdershins Academy—"*

That was when she stopped reading. *Widdershins Academy?* But she hadn't applied there. She hadn't even known it existed!

The phone rang. It was Teddy, sounding shaken. "I'm coming right over," she said, and hung up.

The phone rang again. "Beatrice, it's Ollie." He could barely speak.

"Teddy's on her way," Beatrice said. "Stop by and get Cyrus, okay?"

Fifteen minutes later, the four were sitting in Beatrice's living room in a state of shock. They had all been accepted by Widdershins Academy and not one of them had ever heard of it.

"I sent for catalogues from every senior academy in the Sphere," Teddy said. "At least, I *thought* I did."

The phone rang again and Beatrice reached for it.

"Hi, Miranda . . . Yes, we got them . . . Oh—That's great . . . No . . . No . . . Um—Widdershins . . . You have? So tell me . . . Oh . . . No, that's okay . . . Yeah, you, too, Miranda . . . Bye."

Teddy's eyes were fixed on Beatrice's face. She looked grim. "Miranda got into Honoria Wagstaffe, didn't she?"

Beatrice nodded.

"I *knew* it!" Teddy beat her fist on the arm of the couch. "Oh, this is so unfair!"

"Has she heard of Widdershins?" Ollie asked.

Beatrice nodded again. "But when I asked her about it, she hemmed and hawed and wouldn't say anything. Except that she was *so* sorry."

"Which means," Teddy said bitterly, "that Widdershins is the worst."

"Let's not jump to conclusions," Ollie said.

"Well, you're the expert in witch history," Teddy said. "Have you ever heard of a famous witch named Widdershins?"

"Actually," Ollie said, "I think *widdershins* is a word, not a name."

30

He walked over to Mr. Bailey's desk and picked up a dictionary.

"Water—weighty—wicket," he muttered as he flipped pages, and then he said, "Here it is. *Widdershins. Moving in a counterclockwise, backward, or wrong direction.*"

"Oh, that's just perfect!" Teddy exploded. "We're going to a *backward* academy. How come that doesn't surprise me?"

"Teddy, don't flip out till we know more about it," Ollie said calmly. "Let's go to Beatrice's room and look it up on the computer."

As it turned out, Widdershins Academy didn't have a hexsite. Honoria Wagstaffe and Delphinius Bellows, and even Mystic Isle, had very impressive sites, but not Widdershins.

"I've gotten some hits, though," Ollie said. "Let's see . . . This one's a chat room . . . kids talking about their schools . . ."

Beatrice was leaning over his shoulder, reading, while Teddy paced the room, wild-eyed. Cyrus stood in the doorway looking dazed.

"Okay," Teddy said curtly, "what does it say? Don't try to spare my feelings—just tell me!"

"This girl goes to Silver Willows Academy," Beatrice said. "She says it has fantastic programs in dance and drama. And another student's bragging about Alasdair Bramwell Academy—"

"I don't *care* about those," Teddy wailed. "What does it say about Widdershins?"

When Beatrice and Ollie didn't answer, Teddy marched over to the computer and bent down to look at the screen herself.

"As long as I don't have to go to that awful Widdershins," Teddy read under her breath. *"Everyone knows that's where they send you if you can't make it anywhere else."*

After the initial shock had worn off, Beatrice tried to be philosophical about it. At least she'd still be with Ollie, Teddy, and Cyrus, and that made the idea of leaving home a little less wrenching. Teddy was devastated, of course, moaning about her life being over and suggesting that they just go ahead and put her out of her misery now. Ollie was being stoic, as Beatrice would have expected, but his family was outraged. Imagine, a Tibbs going to a place like *that!* And Cyrus just seemed—well, terrified. Any mention of the school and he started to tremble.

When the moaning and trembling and general disappointment didn't seem to be easing up, Mrs. Bailey contacted Aura Featherstone and asked if she could stop by. So three days after Christmas, Beatrice, Teddy, Ollie, and Cyrus met with Dr. Featherstone in the Baileys' living room.

"I have to admit I'm a little surprised," Dr. Featherstone said, then added hastily, "not that Widdershins is a *bad* school. It's just not one of the better-known ones. In fact, I don't know *anything* about it except that it's in the city of Arcana."

Cyrus had been sitting on the couch beside Beatrice and Cayenne, studying his feet, but now his head jerked up.

"Could you repeat that?" he asked softly. "The city's name?"

"Arcana," Dr. Featherstone said again, giving Cyrus a curious look. "Have you heard of it?"

"No . . . I don't think so," Cyrus answered, but he seemed puzzled by something.

"I would have been amazed if you had," Dr. Featherstone said, "because even witches living in the Sphere aren't that familiar with it, since no one ever goes there."

But Teddy didn't care about Arcana. "You mean, you don't know anything about Widdershins?" she asked impatiently. "Its academic standing? Its field of study?"

"Sorry," Dr. Featherstone said, shaking her head. "But that doesn't mean anything. No one outside the Department of Witch Education knows much about any of the academies unless they've gone there themselves. The headmasters and headmistresses are given a lot of freedom to make their own policies and design the curricula for their individual schools. I do know that Hodge Cadwallader is headmaster at Widdershins, and he's said to be brilliant. He used to have papers in the witch psychology journals all the time, but I haven't heard anything about him in a while."

"So what's Arcana like?" Ollie asked.

"Big and modern—not very different from cities in the mortal world."

"But you said no one ever goes there," Beatrice said. "Why is that?"

Dr. Featherstone hesitated, then said in a casual voice, "Oh, there was some trouble a few years back, but I think that's been taken care of."

Teddy's expression was wary. "What *kind* of trouble? If you're about to tell us there's another Dally Rumpe out there—"

"There was only one Dally Rumpe," Dr. Featherstone said crisply. "But this *is* the Witches' Sphere we're talking about, Teddy. It's *filled* with dark spirits and nightmarish creatures." And then, noticing the uneasy looks they were giving one another, she added, "All right, if you must know, Arcana has its own nightmare. About ten years ago, I guess, this *horror* crawled up out of the earth and started terrorizing the city."

"A *horror*," Beatrice repeated faintly.

"Exactly," Dr. Featherstone said. "And I'm afraid I can't be any more specific than that because no one has actually *seen* the thing—and lived to tell about it."

Teddy opened her mouth to speak, then shut it abruptly and slumped down in her chair.

Dr. Featherstone sighed. "It shouldn't affect the four of you at all, but I'll tell you the little I know about it. You see, beneath Arcana is a maze of natural tunnels and caverns—stretching for miles!—that were carved out eons ago by a river that's since dried up. Well, one day some city workers were down in the tunnels—

inspecting water pipes or something—and that's when they saw it. Sort of. This massive, dark *thing* came rising up out of one of the caverns. The workers said it was as big as a three-story building, and giving off this hideous odor of rotting flesh—but worse than that, smelling of evil and death." Looking around at their wide-eyed faces, she shrugged and added, "I'm just telling you what I read in the paper."

"So the workers *did* see it," Ollie said.

"Not clearly," Dr. Featherstone replied. "It was too dark, and besides, they were mostly interested in getting the heck out of there."

"So did it come after them?" Beatrice asked. "You said it crawled up out of the earth and terrorized the city."

"That came later," Dr. Featherstone said. "When the workers ran back screaming in terror to City Hall, the mayor sent a team of witches into the caverns to destroy the thing. But the witches never came back. Then, that night, all the lights in Arcana suddenly went out and the residents heard a deafening roar and felt the city begin to shake. It was like an earthquake, they said, with whole buildings caving in. But it was actually just that—*atrocity*—crawling up through the tunnels and then coming out into the city. Reports said, in that one night, the creature carried off dozens of innocent witches—presumably to eat, but also, I think, to teach the city a lesson."

"This doesn't sound good at all," Teddy muttered.

"The worst part is, the thing has intelligence," Dr. Featherstone went on. "It can think and plan. It can use magic."

"How do you know that?" Beatrice asked.

"Because it placed an enchantment over Arcana so that no one living there could leave. When they stepped outside the city limits, they were frozen in place. So the mayor sent a second team into the caverns, then a third, and a fourth. But, each time, the team never came back and that creature surfaced again and made off with more witches. Finally, the mayor decided to leave it alone, except for providing raw meat to appease it."

"And that's it?" Ollie asked. "They're just living there with that thing right below them? Can't the government do something?"

"As I've told you," Dr. Featherstone said impatiently, "we have malevolent forces all over the Sphere. The government can't go after all of them. And besides, Arcana hasn't been in the news for ages, so I assume the city has everything under control."

"But how do the people get food and clothes and other things they need?" Ollie persisted.

"Deliveries are still made," Dr. Featherstone said, "but only during daylight hours. And, for obvious reasons, there aren't any visitors to the city. The only new arrivals from year to year are Widdershins students."

"But if Widdershins is in Arcana," Beatrice said, "then once we're there, we'll never be able to leave."

"No, no," Dr. Featherstone said quickly. "The only ones affected by the spell are the witches who were there when the enchantment was put in place. You'll be able to come and go whenever you like. And the campus is protected by sophisticated magic. A report that came out several years ago confirmed that students are perfectly safe on academy grounds." She paused before adding, "The mayor seems to have dealt effectively with the dangers, but I'd still advise you not to leave campus."

"I don't suppose you could get us transferred," Teddy said. "To another academy? Like . . . Oh, I don't know . . . maybe Honoria Wagstaffe?"

Dr. Featherstone looked at her steadily. "I have no authority in this area, Teddy. So I suggest that you find a way to make it work."

4

The Soothsayer

Beatrice stood in the yard with Cayenne in her arms, watching as the Berrys and Tibbses and Rascallions unloaded trunks, computer cases, and backpacks from their SUVs. It was a cold January day, but the sun was shining. Beatrice's last morning in the mortal world promised to be a beautiful one.

Those distressing letters from Widdershins had informed them that neither robes nor uniforms would be required. "You may wear your own clothing, but keep in mind that it must be inoffensive and appropriate for the classroom," the letters had said. Naturally, Teddy had fretted for days over what might be *appropriate*, but Beatrice noticed now that she had on jeans and a heavy jacket like the rest of them.

It seemed that Beatrice's friends had arrived at the Bailey house that morning feeling nostalgic for all things mortal. Munching on a bagel with cream cheese, Cyrus had remarked sadly, "I guess I won't be having one of these again for a while." And Ollie had commented that he'd really been looking forward to the next *Masterpiece Theatre* on PBS. "Remember when I bought these boots at the mall?" Teddy had asked

Beatrice in a subdued voice. "Forty percent off. Some of the best moments of my life have been spent at that mall."

Now it was almost time for them to leave. Teddy's parents and little brother, Rupert, were hugging her. Ollie's father was giving him last-minute advice on how to conduct himself in the Sphere, while Mrs. Tibbs stroked Ollie's hair and blinked back tears. And Cyrus's parents were holding on to their son for dear life, with Mrs. Rascallion murmuring, "We're so proud of you," and Mr. Rascallion nodding and swallowing hard.

Beatrice's mother and father came to stand on either side of her.

"Well, this is it," Mr. Bailey said, his voice a little too hearty.

"Did you check your closet again?" Mrs. Bailey asked brightly. "Of course, if you forgot anything, I can mail it to you. I wish we could call you, or at least send e-mails to the Sphere. But we can write. And summer vacation's just around the corner."

"That's true," Beatrice said, doing her best to produce a convincing smile. "I'll be back before you know it, Mom."

And that was when she saw the old wreck of a bus pulling up to the curb. It was mostly a sickly green color, except for the one gray fender and rust spots, and on the side was painted *Happy Hills Academy*. For the benefit of their mortal neighbors, Beatrice assumed, but—*Happy Hills?* How lame was that?

"This is so embarrassing," Teddy muttered.

The door to the bus screeched open and a scrawny man wearing ill-fitting mortal clothes clumped down the steps. Beatrice took in the orange parka that was two sizes too large, the green checked pants that didn't quite reach his ankles, and the purple knit cap with a pom-pom on top. *Oh, yeah*, she thought, *he won't be noticed by the neighbors in that getup.*

"Merry meet," the bus driver said, but there was nothing merry in his expression. He was all business. "My name is Toogood Mars. I'm Dr. Cadwallader's personal assistant." He puffed up with self-importance and his glasses slid down his skinny nose. He jabbed them back into place and added, "I'm here to take you all to—um, Happy Hills Academy. So let's get going. I'm on a schedule."

Everyone snapped into action, carrying trunks and bags over to the bus and stowing them in the side compartment. Then there were more hugs and final instructions, and Beatrice and her friends were boarding the bus.

It was practically empty. A boy was napping in a seat up front, and a girl was sitting about halfway back, hunched over a book. She didn't appear to notice when Beatrice and Ollie sat down across from her and Teddy and Cyrus took the seat behind them.

Beatrice unzipped her jacket and placed Cayenne on her lap. While the others got settled, she stole a glance across the aisle. The girl was wearing a gray cardigan and a pleated skirt—dorky even by mortal standards—and everything about her was thin, from her bony arms and legs to her wispy, sand-colored hair. She was the kind of girl who blended in, quiet, shy, not wanting to draw attention to herself. But there was tension in her face, a strained look that made Beatrice wonder about her. And how could a book that thick and moldy-looking be so riveting?

Toogood Mars bounded up the steps, shut the door, and took his seat. He snapped his fingers and the bus sprang to life. As it sputtered and chugged, Beatrice looked outside where their moms and dads were gathered in a sad-looking huddle, waving. She and her friends waved back.

Then the bus started rattling down the street, jolting them up and down, and Beatrice wondered if it would even make it to the corner, much less all the way to the Witches' Sphere. She turned around in her seat and craned her neck to catch one last glimpse of her parents.

The bus left town and hit the interstate. Teddy leaned forward and said in an anxious voice, "I wonder if I remembered to pack my red mittens. I read on the Web that it's winter in Arcana, too, and I'll need those mittens."

Ollie turned around and gave her a look, as if he couldn't believe she was worrying about *mittens*. Then he opened a book titled *The Werewolf Rebellion of 1362* and started to read.

41

Beatrice glanced back at Cyrus, who was staring out the window, and at Teddy, who was now digging frantically in the pockets of her jacket, apparently in search of mittens. No one seemed to be in the mood to talk, so Beatrice turned her attention to their fellow travelers.

The boy was still asleep. When they were boarding, Beatrice had thought he looked older, maybe fifteen or sixteen. Now all she could see was his spiky hair and one long, blue-jeaned leg stuck out into the aisle.

The girl across from them had finally lifted her head and was sitting there with her eyes shut, muttering under her breath. Then she looked down at the book with a desperate air, grimaced, and closed her eyes again.

Beatrice was wondering if she planned on memorizing all two thousand pages of that book, when, all of a sudden, the bus swerved onto an off-ramp and pulled into a small town. Careening down a residential street, it came to an abrupt stop in front of a yellow house. A boy was hugging a woman—his mother, Beatrice assumed—while a man dragged a trunk over to the bus. The boy looked like half the guys at Beatrice's middle school, a little on the short side, with brown hair that could use a trim. He had a basketball and a backpack with a big tube sticking out of it, the kind used for storing maps.

Beatrice watched as the boy loped over to the bus and sprang lightly up the steps. He stood there looking down the rows of seats, his eyes landing on the reader-girl before moving on to Beatrice and her friends. Then he started down the aisle, but he'd only taken a couple of steps when he tripped over the foot of the boy up front. The backpack fell off his shoulder and the cardboard tube dropped out and rolled, scattering its contents. Beatrice saw some big sheets of paper with lines and squiggles that looked more like diagrams than maps.

Ollie got up to help him retrieve his stuff, but the boy was already on his hands and knees, scrambling for the papers. He jerked one of them out of Ollie's hand, as if he didn't want anyone seeing it. Beatrice wondered what *that* was all about.

The bus had started to move by the time he'd rolled up his diagrams and slid them back into the tube. He continued down the aisle and flopped into the seat in front of Beatrice and Ollie.

Twisting around, the boy grinned and said to Ollie, "Thanks for your help." Then he looked at Beatrice and added, "Hi, I'm Kick Tazwell."

"Beatrice Bailey."

"Yeah, I know," he said cheerfully. "I've seen your picture in *Enchantment News*—and just about every other magazine and newspaper in the Sphere." His eyes moving from face to face, he said, "And you're Ollie, right? And you two are Teddy and Cyrus, and the cat's Cayenne."

"That's right," Ollie said, looking uncomfortable. He still wasn't used to being a celebrity.

"Hey, I didn't mean to embarrass you," Kick said, "but you are pretty famous, with all that Dally Rumpe business. There's just one thing I don't understand."

"What's that?" Beatrice asked, already deciding that she liked him.

"Well, since you're on this old clunker they call a bus, you must be going to Widdershins. But my question is, *Why?* When you could've gone anywhere. All the witch academies must've been fighting to get you."

"Famous or not," Beatrice said, "we're not very good at magic. One spell each, that's it. So I guess the academies *weren't* fighting over us."

"I can't even cast one spell and have it work right," Kick said, "but that's okay. I'd rather play basketball anytime."

"You can do that in the mortal world," Ollie said. "Why go to a witch academy at all?"

"Because my parents want to be sure that I'm ready to live my whole life as a mortal," Kick replied. "So I agreed to give this witch thing a chance and try an academy for two years." He grinned again. "I just didn't expect it to be Widdershins. But one more year and I can come back home and forget all this."

"But the academies only take Classical witches," Teddy said, "so you must have done *something* magical to prove yourself."

"When the Witches' Executive Committee classified me, they said I was a soothsayer." Kick shrugged. "I don't know about that, but sometimes I can predict things that are going to happen. Like, one day, I had this image in my head of my dad locking up his hardware store, and somehow I knew he was going to have to close down for good. And, sure enough, a few months later, this big chain built a discount store in town and it ran my dad out of business."

Teddy looked impressed and maybe a little envious. "I wouldn't mind being able to see into the future," she said.

"No? Well, I'd give it up in a minute if I could," Kick said. "Then I wouldn't be wasting my time at Widdershins."

"It's a school for losers, right?"

"*Ted-dy.*" Beatrice shot her a stern look.

But Kick seemed to be giving Teddy's question serious thought. "Some people see it that way," he said, "and others don't."

"What is this, a riddle?" Teddy asked irritably. "Just tell us about Widdershins."

Kick glanced at the girl across the aisle and said in a low voice, "Actually, we're not supposed to tell new students about the academy. Not till Cadwallader talks to them."

"Cadwallader," Ollie said. "That's the headmaster."

"Right," Kick said. "And he wants to be the one to tell you about the school, and why you've been brought there."

"So there's a reason?" Teddy asked flippantly. "Besides us being incompetent, I mean."

Kick hesitated, cutting his eyes at the book-girl again, and then he said, "All I can tell you is, every student at Widdershins is handpicked by Dr. Cadwallader. And it has to do with talent—not the lack of it."

Beatrice knew that Teddy would keep grilling him, and Kick must have reached the same conclusion because he added hastily, "If I say any more, and

Cadwallader finds out, I'll be in detention till summer break."

As he spoke, Beatrice realized that they were sinking into darkness. Before long, she couldn't see anything, but it felt like the bus had risen off the road and was flying through the air. Then, within seconds, they hit solid ground again. And hit *hard!* Beatrice's body jerked back on impact and Cayenne's claws dug into her hand as the cat struggled to hold on.

"Wow," Teddy said, and let out a shaky breath. "*Somebody* needs to learn how to land this thing."

"Oh, that was one of the softer landings," Kick said through the darkness, and Beatrice could hear the smile in his voice.

"So tell us, O Great Soothsayer," Teddy said, "what do you see in our futures at the backward academy?"

"Sorry," Kick said, "but I can't make predictions any time I want to."

"Well, I have a prediction," Cyrus said into the darkness. "I predict that we're going to wish we'd never come to this place."

There was a fierceness in his voice that Beatrice found unsettling. "Cyrus," she said, more sharply than she'd intended, "are you trying to creep us out?"

"I'm just telling you what I think," Cyrus shot back.

Beatrice was feeling uneasy. Maybe he was having a nervous breakdown. Or maybe there really was something ominous waiting for them at Widdershins. But how could Cyrus possibly know that?

5

Widdershins Academy

S unlight had broken through the darkness, and just ahead, they could see an urban skyline. Arcana was just as Dr. Featherstone had described it, a metropolis of tall, modern buildings that spread out for miles. Beatrice noticed that even the girl across the aisle had lifted her head to look.

"It seems okay," Ollie said, "not like a city under siege."

And not like the Witches' Sphere, either, Beatrice thought. But before she could say anything, Cyrus blurted out, "It isn't okay! We should go home—before it's too late!"

Startled, everyone turned to look at him. Beatrice saw that all the color had drained from his face and sweat glistened on his forehead.

"Cyrus?" She leaned toward him. "Are you all right?"

But he was staring into space and didn't respond.

"Cyrus!"

His head jerked toward Teddy's voice, and then he blinked, as if surprised to see her there.

"Cyrus, what just happened?" Beatrice asked. "Where were you?"

He gave her a bewildered look and answered, "I don't know what you're talking about."

They were all trying to act as if nothing unusual had happened, but Beatrice couldn't help stealing a glance at Cyrus as the bus pulled onto the six-lane highway that led into the city. A highway, Beatrice soon realized, with hardly any traffic. She counted five vehicles besides the bus, all of them bright and shiny, but looking like they might have just rolled out of an antique auto show.

Watching her, Kick said, "That's the kind of car they drive around here. Phantoms and Nymphs. They're spell-driven, don't use gas at all."

"But what's the point of six lanes for five cars?" she asked.

"They say there used to be lots of traffic," Kick said. "But you've heard about the monster, right? Well, it doesn't do much for tourism."

From a distance, Arcana had looked clean and shining, but as they entered the city, Beatrice could see that it was neglected. Trash littered the streets and most of the windows were coated with a layer of grime. Even more unsightly were the empty lots, where all that remained of the buildings that had once stood there were brick foundations or charred half walls—grim reminders of the city's nights of terror, Beatrice assumed.

Then she noticed how quiet it was. Eerily so. A red-and-yellow streetcar crossed the intersection in front of them, but there was no other traffic on the street, except for a few witches riding by on broomsticks. And there weren't many pedestrians, either. Arcana was a huge city, supposedly crammed full of witches unable to leave. So where were they?

"It's like a ghost town," she said.

"People are used to staying inside," Kick said. "Just because that thing has never come up during the day, doesn't mean it can't."

Beatrice was eager to hear what Kick knew about the creature and turned to ask him. But suddenly the bus started to vibrate. Then it lurched toward the sidewalk, and Beatrice thought, *Toogood Mars could really use some driving lessons.*

It wasn't until Ollie exclaimed, "Hey! What's going on?" that she looked out the window and realized that the bus had jumped the curb and come to a stop. But it was still shaking! And that's when she noticed that all the buildings around them were swaying.

"Oh, my gosh!" Teddy shouted. "It's that—*thing*—the monster!"

Beatrice swiveled her head to look out the other side of the bus, but all she saw were brooms tossed to the pavement and the desperate faces of witches as they ran, stumbling, while the street shook under their feet.

It was terrible! Like being trapped in the center of an earthquake, only worse. Because the real horror was what was lurking beneath the shuddering asphalt, something too frightening to imagine, much less encounter face-to-face. And at this very moment, it might be crawling up out of the earth!

And then, just as suddenly as it started, the shaking stopped. Beatrice let out a ragged breath and glanced around at her friends. They looked as scared as she was. Only Kick seemed calm. And resigned.

"Does this happen all the time?" Teddy demanded.

"Often enough," Kick said, "only it's always been at night till now. So we aren't allowed to leave campus after dark. That's when witches disappear and are never heard from again."

"What *is* this monstrosity, anyway?" Teddy asked. "People must have some idea."

Kick shrugged. "I don't think so. They just know that it's huge and dark and evil."

Toogood Mars had started up the bus again, and Beatrice was murmuring to an indignant Cayenne, who didn't take well to being shaken, when suddenly the bus door slammed open. Beatrice's head jerked forward as a tall figure bounded up the steps, followed by three others, all of them wearing dark robes with hoods that hid their faces.

The girl across the aisle whimpered and the boy up front dove to the floor. Toogood Mars rose out of his seat, looking shocked and angry, but then one of the intruders raised an arm and pointed a finger at the bus driver. Instantly, Toogood slumped into his seat and began to mumble and snicker and gaze senselessly into space.

Beatrice had no idea who the intruders were, or what they wanted, but it was obvious that everyone on the bus was in danger. And with Toogood under some kind of spell that had left him giggly and goofy, there was no one to protect them.

One of the strangers came striding down the aisle—and then stopped beside Beatrice. The next thing she knew, strong hands grabbed her shoulders, pulling her out of her seat. At the same moment, Ollie jumped up and lunged at the hooded figure, while Cayenne flew at the attacker's face. Beatrice heard a scream of pain and the hands on her shoulders loosened their grip enough for her to wrestle free. After that, everything happened so fast, she had only a blurred impression of the hooded figure striking out and of Cyrus grabbing hold of the dark robe and muttering something under his breath. Then she heard the words, "Cut him down to inches three, as my will so mote it be," and she knew what Cyrus had done.

When the other robed figures saw the diminutive size of their companion, they started backing up the aisle—and then they ran, followed by their tiny accomplice. Everyone crowded around Beatrice, asking if she was all right, while Beatrice cuddled Cayenne and reassured herself that the cat wasn't hurt. Then they checked on Toogood Mars, who was still sitting in the driver's seat, but no longer giggling, and looking around with a dazed expression as if just waking up from a dream.

"He doesn't even know what happened," Beatrice said.

"Well, neither do I!" Teddy exclaimed. "Who were those guys?"

"Someone trying to get Beatrice off this bus," Ollie said grimly.

Beatrice's pounding heart sped up a notch at that. "You're sure it was me, *specifically*, they were after?" she asked weakly. "Maybe they just wanted to rob us."

"That's not good," Ollie said, "but better than attempted kidnapping, I guess. We'll have to report this to Dr. Cadwallader."

The boy up front was gaping at them, while the book-girl huddled in her seat, trembling. Still calm, Kick was looking steadily at Beatrice. "So you don't know anyone who'd want to kidnap you?"

"What for, the fifty-seven dollars in my bank account?" She managed a shaky smile. "I think they just happened to grab me first. And thanks to Ollie and Cyrus and Cayenne, their plans to rob us didn't work." She turned to Cyrus and added, "That spell of yours couldn't have been better timed. Thanks, Cyrus."

Scowling, he said, "Didn't I tell you we shouldn't have come here?"

Just then, the bus started moving. Oblivious to everything that had happened, Toogood Mars backed into the street and took off. In the middle of the next block, he pulled up to a pair of black wrought-iron gates that had a large *W* worked into their intricate design. But rust had eaten away the paint, and the gates seemed to be a forlorn remnant of happier days.

"I never thought I'd be glad to see Widdershins," Kick said. "And there are two of our guards. Where are they when you need them?"

Beatrice didn't see any guards, but as the gates swung open, she noticed two tiny, fairylike creatures fluttering above them. They were about the size of butterflies.

Ollie raised an eyebrow. "We have *fairies* for guards?"

"A special *kind* of fairy called sky dancers," Kick said. "They make sure we don't do anything stupid, like leaving school grounds after dark."

That was when Beatrice noticed that the book-girl, still trembling a little, was actually looking at them. Before she could duck back into her book, Beatrice said quickly, "Hi, I'm Beatrice Bailey."

The girl blinked and her cheeks turned pink. She mumbled something and dropped her head.

"Sorry," Beatrice said, "I didn't hear you."

The girl's eyes darted back to Beatrice's face. "I'm Iris Tinker," she repeated softly, but loud enough this time for Beatrice to hear.

She seemed painfully shy and Beatrice wanted to put her at ease. But then Kick said, "You don't want to miss this. First sight of old Widdershins."

The bus was rattling down a long, gravel drive that was lined with leafless trees. Dirty snow was piled up on either side, with patches of brown lawn peeking through.

"I don't see—" Beatrice started, and then stopped. Because at the end of the drive, she did see.

It was a gray stone house with a slate roof and lots of chimneys. As the bus moved closer, Beatrice realized just how huge the place was. And how old. Carvings along the eaves and over the windows had crumbled to the point that the original design was unrecognizable, except for the occasional gargoyle or sharp-fanged serpent glaring down at them. Stone steps rose up to meet massive wooden doors, and above them was a sign painted in tarnished gold on black that read: *Widdershins Academy*.

"Oh. My. Gosh," Teddy whispered. "It's worse than I'd imagined."

"But—*interesting*, don't you think?" Ollie said, the look of dismay on his face contradicting his words.

The bus stopped in front of the steps, which Beatrice could now see were also crumbling, and Toogood Mars looked over his shoulder at them.

"Go on inside while I get your bags," he said. "You old boys can take the new ones up to the dorm, can't you?" He pulled a sheet of paper out of his pocket and glanced at it. "Rathbone and Tazwell, you'll have your same rooms. Tibbs is in 411 and Rascallion's in 413. You girls wait in the front hall."

"First robbers and now this," Teddy was muttering. "It's a dump. And you know it's got to be haunted. I won't be able to sleep a wink."

But it wasn't a ghost that watched as they disembarked from the bus. Draperies at a second-floor window stirred slightly, and had they looked up, Beatrice and her companions would have seen a face behind the glass. A face that was very much alive. But no one noticed the shadowy figure in the window. And, certainly, no one heard the watcher whisper in near-frenzied excitement, "I've waited so long, but it's finally going to happen. Now that *she's* here. Welcome to Widdershins Academy, Beatrice Bailiwick."

6

The Bane Project

Beatrice's heart was thumping again as she followed Teddy up the front steps. Iris had edged
in close beside her, more timid than ever. The
doors creaked open unassisted and they entered a cav-
ernous front hall that had dark stone walls and floors.
And no heat. Beatrice shivered. It was colder in there
than outside and smelled of dust and mildew.

There was an arched doorway in each of the four
walls and a wide, stone staircase leading to the upper
floors. Hanging from the ceiling was a chandelier about
the size of a compact car, draped in cobwebs and holding hundreds of candles. Only most of them had burned
down to nubs, and the faint light from the few remain-
ing tapers left the corners in shadow.

Teddy peered up at the chandelier. "No electricity?"

"Not since the monster knocked it out," Kick said.
"They'd have to go down under the city to fix it and no
one's volunteering to do that. But we have lights in our
rooms and in the classrooms. Spell-powered."

Beatrice had walked over to look at the one and
only painting in the room. It was a grim, if realistic, por-

trayal of this house, done mostly in shades of gray. *About as welcoming as the real thing,* she thought.

Everyone else had congregated in the center of the room, except for the boy who'd been napping on the bus. He was slumped against the wall near Beatrice, and now that he was standing, she could see that he had the meaty build of a wrestler and a plump-cheeked face with small, dark eyes.

Kick sidled up to the boy and said, "Hi, Axel. How was break?"

Axel shrugged. "Okay, I guess. But I can't wait to leave the mortal world for good."

"Don't you graduate this year? Then you'll be able to move to the Sphere and be on your own."

The boy shrugged again. "Cadwallader's threatening to flunk me if I don't—to use his words—*dazzle* him with my fieldwork. If he'd just assign me to the Bane Project—" Then he caught himself and added in a low voice, "You know he's made up the assignments list. I'd sure like to see it."

Frowning, Kick said softly, "Come on, Axel, do you really want to work on the Bane Project—and get yourself killed?"

Beatrice froze. Did he say *killed?* What *was* this project, anyway?

Looking sullen now, Axel said, "That's funny, coming from you, since you're bound to be working on it."

Kick's eyes dropped to the floor. "We don't know that," he muttered.

"Sure we do. You're Cadwallader's pet—now that Milo's gone."

Kick's head jerked up and he was about to say something, but Axel cut him off. "Look, man, I know what you're planning—and it's a whole lot riskier than me working on the Bane Project. But if *you'll* help *me*, I might be able to help you, too."

Kick eyed him warily. "Help you how?"

"I just want to get my hands on that assignments sheet," Axel said. "And I'll bet you know where Cadwallader keeps it. Milo told you everything."

Kick hesitated, apparently torn, but about that time Ollie and Cyrus walked up. Kick looked surprised, as if he'd forgotten all about them.

"Oh—we were supposed to take you up to the dorm," Kick said, sounding flustered. "Um—this is Axel Rathbone. He and I have something to do, but you won't have any trouble finding your rooms. Just take those stairs up to the fourth floor."

Ollie said, "Sure," and then he came over to Beatrice. "Meet us down here later," he said. "We can take a walk and look around."

Cyrus gave the girls a listless wave and followed Ollie to the stairs, dragging his backpack behind him.

Watching them climb the stairs, Beatrice suddenly felt lonely and miserable. At that moment, she would have given anything to be back home. She missed her parents. She even missed her mother's terrible French toast. Then she noticed Iris standing there, looking lost and scared, and Beatrice felt ashamed for giving in to self-pity. She had Cayenne and her three best friends here with her, while Iris had no one.

But about that time Beatrice saw Kick and Axel disappear through one of the arched doorways, and without pausing to think about it, she tucked Cayenne into her jacket and went after them. The boys were walking quickly down a long, dimly lit hallway. Keeping her distance, Beatrice followed.

Kick and Axel passed several darkened rooms and then stopped in front of a closed door. Pressing her body against the wall, Beatrice watched as Kick opened the door and slipped inside, with Axel on his heels. When Beatrice reached the door, she saw a tarnished brass plaque that read *Hodge Cadwallader, Headmaster*, and all of a sudden she had a very bad feeling about this.

The boys had left the door ajar and Beatrice peeked inside. It was a small, shadowy office, with a wooden desk in the center and some chairs lined up against the wall. Behind the desk was a second doorway that Kick and Axel were now passing through.

Beatrice heard Axel say softly, "It's dark in here."

"There's a candle on Cadwallader's desk," Kick whispered back.

A few seconds later, the inner office was filled with soft, flickering light. Still poised in the outer doorway, Beatrice saw Kick move over to a large desk that was covered with stacks of books and pull on a drawer.

"It's locked," he said.

"Where do you think he keeps the key?"

"Probably in his pocket."

"Are you sure the list would be in the desk?" Axel asked.

"Milo said he kept all the paperwork on the Bane Project in this top drawer," Kick answered. "Sorry. But we can't break the lock. He'd know."

"Well, I'm not giving up yet," Axel said. "Is that cabinet locked?"

He and Kick disappeared from sight and Beatrice heard a drawer slide open. She took that opportunity to slip into the outer office and crouch down on the far side of the desk, where they wouldn't see her when they left.

Then she heard Kick say, "This is just budget stuff . . . orders for textbooks . . . school calendars . . . Come on, let's get out of here."

"Just a minute," Axel said. "And, anyway, you should be as interested in finding that list as I am."

"Why should *I* care?"

"We both know why," Axel said gruffly. "You may have fooled everybody else, but I know what you're up to, Kick."

Beatrice heard a drawer slam shut, and then . . . another sound. Footsteps. Someone was coming down the hall!

She ducked lower behind the desk, heart pounding as the footsteps moved closer and closer—till they stopped just outside the office. Suddenly the candle went out, leaving the room in near darkness. And then the outer door creaked all the way open.

Beatrice didn't dare look up, so she couldn't see what was happening, but all at once there was movement nearby. Someone was walking through the doorway, just as Kick and Axel came barreling out of the other office.

Then Kick said in a high, thin voice, "Oh—Dr. Cadwallader. We were looking for you. Came by to say hi."

There was no response, just a heavy silence in the room, then a noise like a throaty growl and a deep voice saying, "Is that *so*? You come into a dark office expecting to find me? A *private* office, I might add."

Beatrice could tell from the man's tone that he didn't believe Kick. He sounded suspicious, even angry. It was obvious that he didn't like finding the boys here one bit. So how would he react if he looked behind the desk and saw her huddled there? And what if he went into his office to work? She'd never be able to get out of here without him seeing her.

Then Axel said, "Well, I'm sure you're busy, Dr. Cadwallader, so we won't keep you. It's—um—good to be back. Looking forward to the new semester."

"For Pete's sake, Rathbone, don't play up to me," the headmaster snapped. "The only thing that impresses me is *excellence*. And from what I've seen of your work, thus far, you have a long way to go. Now, get out of here, both of you. I have work of my own to do."

Beatrice very nearly groaned at that, but then Dr. Cadwallader said, "On second thought, I'll see you out myself, just to make sure you're where you're *supposed* to be."

Beatrice waited about a minute after she heard them leave the office. Then she stood up, and holding a hand on Cayenne to keep her from jumping down, tiptoed to the doorway and peeked outside. The corridor was empty.

When she walked into the front hall, Beatrice found Teddy and Iris still standing there.

"Where have you *been?*" Teddy demanded, giving Beatrice a look that was clearly annoyed. "Toogood Mars came in with our trunks and told us he was sending someone down to take us to our rooms. But that was *ages* ago."

Ignoring her friend's bad mood, Beatrice said to Iris, "So you've met Teddy? And the boys are Ollie and Cyrus. I'll introduce you to them later."

Iris looked at Beatrice, then Teddy, and back again, blinking fast. "I heard that boy—Kick, is that his name? I heard him mention your pictures being in the paper, and then I remembered. My mom and dad get *The Specter* mailed to them and I read some articles about you. You've done incredible things."

"Mostly luck," Beatrice said lightly. "Believe me, we're all magically challenged."

Now Teddy was regarding Iris with interest. "*You* must be good at magic for them to make you Classical," she said.

Iris shook her head, looking embarrassed. "I can't cast spells at all. The Witches' Executive Committee said they'd classified me Classical because of—well, some healing work I've done."

"You mean, like making warts go away?" Teddy asked.

"Yes . . . and curing burns and broken arms. Things like that."

Beatrice and Teddy were staring at her in astonishment.

"Wait a minute," Teddy said. "You can *cure* broken arms? Without casts? On the spot?"

"Usually," Iris said. "It's just a matter of thinking hard about the bone mending while you rest your hands on the break. It's nothing, really."

"Sounds like something to me," Beatrice said.

Now Iris looked even more embarrassed, but pleased, too.

"Do you have any idea why you were sent to Widdershins and not one of the other academies?" Teddy asked her.

Iris shook her head. "But I heard what Kick told you, that we've been handpicked by the headmaster, and for a specific reason. So there must be at least one thing we all have in common."

Beatrice was anxious to tell them what she'd overheard about the Bane Project—and to ask what they thought of Kick—but just then, an old woman with a broom came shuffling into the hall. She was wearing soot-covered robes and her gray hair was thick and matted, hanging nearly to her ankles and resembling a dirty animal pelt.

The woman began to sweep the stone floor and clouds of dust billowed up, settling elsewhere, but mostly on Beatrice, Teddy, and Iris. When Teddy sneezed, the sweeper raised her head and gave them an ill-humored look.

"If it bothers you, move away," she hissed, like an angry snake.

The three girls stepped back, but the woman continued to glare at them. "In case you're wondering," she said, "I'm not a witch. I'm a fairy from the dark side of the Sphere. Oh, I see you're surprised. You're used to those dainty, little bits of fluff that fly around like gypsy moths. Well, it's a big world and there's room in it for all sorts of fairies. And not that you've asked, but my name is Rhude."

Beatrice was thinking this seemed like an appropriate name for her when a second, nearly identical woman plodded in with a pail of water and a mop. She, too, was less than clean and had the same matted hair— only some was missing on one side and she looked rather washed-out and wispy.

"You're a ghost," Beatrice said, and then wondered if it was discourteous to mention it.

"This is Rankin, my sister," Rhude said, "and, yes, she's only with us in spirit now—ever since that dragon attacked our barrow and crushed poor Rankin with one stomp of his foot. And before that, he breathed on her and burned half her hair off. In case you happened to notice. But . . . it's all turned out for the best."

"Easy for you to say!" Rankin spat out the words in that same hissing voice. "You're not *dead!*"

Turning her glare on her sister, Rhude said, "Don't I help you with your haunting and all?"

Then she looked back at Beatrice. "When we started working here, there wasn't a single ghost—can you imagine?—so Rankin had to get busy. And since the place is too big to haunt alone, I do my best to pitch in."

"Um—that's very nice of you," Beatrice said. "I'm sure Rankin appreciates it."

"Not that I've noticed," Rhude replied.

"What I'd *appreciate*," Rankin informed her, "is going back home. Too much happening here that's not quite right, and you know it."

Rhude spun around to face her sister. "Watch your mouth, you old fairy-crone! There's things best left unsaid."

Raising her chin defiantly, Rankin responded, "I don't need you telling me that, so draw in your claws, you ugly old hagfish."

"That's enough, you two," came a voice from the doorway.

A big woman with a broad, red face strode into the hall. Her brown hair was caught up in a silver net that resembled a spider's web, and she had spots down the front of her apron like she'd splashed soup on it. Or maybe, blood. It was hard to tell.

The woman smiled at Beatrice, Teddy, and Iris. "You must be new," she said. "Welcome. I'm Zipporah Spitz, Director of Food Service at Widdershins." Then she added to Rhude and Rankin, "Hadn't you best be getting back to work before Mrs. Harridan comes after you?"

Rhude snarled and muttered, "The old harpy."

But Beatrice noticed that she was already slinking toward a doorway, with Rankin close behind her. Apparently, they didn't want to mess with Mrs. Harridan, whoever she was.

Zipporah was leaving, too, but she stopped and said over her shoulder, "You're welcome in my kitchen any time. Drop by for a snack. Or just to get out of the thick of things."

Then she was gone, leaving them to wonder what she'd meant by *the thick of things*.

"I'm not used to magical creatures," Iris said nervously. "Of course, I've read about them—I've *read* about everything—but seeing sky dancers and dark-side fairies in person is different."

"I know how you feel," Beatrice said, wanting to reassure her. "This is my sixth trip to the Sphere and I still can't keep them all straight."

"Then, perhaps," said a voice from behind them, "you should try harder."

They turned around to see a stern-faced witch in gray robes standing at the bottom of the stairs. There was a regal air about her, from her imposing height to the braid of white hair wrapped around her head like a crown. The woman's pale blue eyes bore into them and Beatrice felt a chill run up her spine. The room had suddenly grown colder.

"I am Mrs. Harridan," the witch said, her voice as frosty as her manner. "Besides being the girls' dorm matron, I see that everything runs smoothly in this house. Now, get your bags and come with me."

She turned and began a slow ascent up the staircase. *Like a queen*, Beatrice thought, *admitting the common folk into her castle.*

The girls fell into step behind the dorm matron and Teddy flashed Beatrice a look that clearly said, *This just gets worse and worse.*

7

This House of Horrors

Mrs. Harridan started down the third-floor corridor.

"The boys are right above us," Teddy whispered to Beatrice.

But Mrs. Harridan heard and whipped around to face them. "It doesn't matter *where* the boys are," she said sharply. "Dorms are strictly off-limits to members of the opposite sex. Is that understood?"

"Yes, ma'am," Teddy said meekly.

Mrs. Harridan gave Beatrice and Iris suspicious looks and then continued down the hall. It was narrow and unadorned except for the few candles in wall brackets that were burning too low to provide much light. Then the witch stopped abruptly at door number 307 and said, "This is your room, Miss Bailiwick."

The woman hadn't asked for their names, but she obviously knew who they were. Beatrice was thinking that Mrs. Harridan was one of those people who made it her business to know *everything*.

With more wariness than anticipation, Beatrice walked into a room that could more appropriately be called a cell. It was just large enough for a cotlike bed, a small dresser, and a desk. At the head of the bed was a window with dark, dusty draperies, and a door stood open to reveal the tiniest closet Beatrice had ever seen.

"You can use the time before dinner to unpack your things," Mrs. Harridan said in her starchy voice. "The bathroom is at the end of the hall. Dinner is served at six. Don't be tardy."

Then the door slammed shut, leaving Beatrice and Cayenne alone.

The cat jumped from Beatrice's arms to the bed. After slowly walking its length, Cayenne stretched out on the faded coverlet—which might have been blue at one time, but was now a dingy gray—and made a sound that was half sigh and half grumble. Beatrice sat down and felt the mattress flatten out under her.

"Okay, so it isn't like the rooms in the catalogs," she said, looking around. "It's small. And dreary. But it's going to be our home now, Cayenne, so we'd better get used to it."

Then she stood up and looked out the window. Their room was at the back of the house and there wasn't much to see, just a deep lawn dotted with leafless trees, and beyond, dense woods.

Beatrice opened her trunk and started to unpack. But the closet and dresser were filled in no time and she ended up piling most of her stuff on the closet floor.

She was closing the trunk lid when she happened to glance out the window again and spotted an animal at the edge of the woods, its coppery fur shimmering against the gray tree trunks. Was it a fox? Maybe, *the* fox? She was too far away to be sure, but it was the right size, the right color. And it was staring up at the house, as if waiting for something. Or someone.

When Beatrice stepped out into the hall, with Cayenne on her shoulder, Teddy and Iris were standing in the adjacent doorway.

"Come on over," Teddy said. "You have to see my new digs."

Beatrice followed her into a tiny room that was identical to her own, down to the faded coverlet and dusty draperies.

"Depressing, huh?" Teddy said. "And have you tried your bed? It's like lying on a concrete slab!"

"But at least we're close together," Iris said. "I'm one door down."

"Well, I don't intend to spend any more time in this cubicle than I have to," Teddy said. "Let's get out of here."

"Ollie and Cyrus are probably waiting for us," Beatrice said. "I just have to get my jacket."

Teddy and Iris waited outside while Beatrice ran into her room—and stopped dead in her tracks. A *boy* was standing at the dresser with his back to her, digging around in her pajama drawer!

"What the—"

But Beatrice didn't finish because the boy spun around, and she saw that it was Kick. He just stared at her, his expression a mixture of surprise and guilt.

"Kick Tazwell!" Beatrice exclaimed. "What do you think you're doing, going through my things?"

"Um—I know this looks bad," he said, taking a tentative step toward her, "but I can explain."

"You'd better," Beatrice said, "and fast."

Teddy and Iris had come to the door and were peering in.

"What are you doing in Beatrice's room?" Teddy asked him.

"Pawing through my stuff," Beatrice said, not taking her eyes off the boy. "And you were going to tell me why," she added coolly to Kick.

"It's—Well, this room—Someone I used to know—" Kick cleared his throat, looking a little desperate. "Aw, heck! I can't tell you what I was doing here, but I *wasn't* stealing! I wasn't doing *anything* wrong!"

"No, just rifling through Beatrice's personal things," Teddy retorted. "And she deserves an explanation."

Kick's face turned pink and then he glared at Teddy. "Well—I'm sorry, but I can't give her one. Not right now, anyway."

Then he stomped past them and took off down the hall.

They all stared after him, astonished, until Iris said in a small voice, "You don't think he *was* stealing. Do you?"

Beatrice shook her head. "I don't know *what* he was doing. I thought he was a good guy, but I'm beginning to think maybe I was wrong."

She got her jacket and they started down the hall, their feet making dull thuds against the stone.

Ducking a spider's web that was hanging from the ceiling, Teddy said, "Maybe it won't seem so creepy once everyone else gets here. No, I take that back. This place will *always* be creepy."

"You've got that right," came a loud voice from the stairwell. Then the speaker turned the corner, loaded down with bags.

It was a girl about their age, but Beatrice had never seen anyone like her. She had long black hair and was wearing a red velvet cape that brushed the floor. Beneath the cape, Beatrice caught a glimpse of a very short skirt and black boots with tall, skinny heels.

As the girl approached them, Beatrice could see that she was pretty—in a flashy sort of way. She was wearing dark red lipstick, black eyeliner, and lots of jewelry—beaded chains around her neck, sparkly rings on most of her fingers, and a silver one through her eyebrow.

The girl came to a stop in front of them. Black eyes narrowed, she stared, assessing them, her gaze lingering longest on Teddy.

Then she said in a voice that was anything but friendly, "I'm Diantha Winter-Rose, back for my third year in this house of horrors. I know, you're all eager little witches who want to astound the world with your brilliance, but that's not going to happen. I can already

72

see, you don't have what it takes. So. Welcome to the worst academy in the Sphere. And I hope you make it through your first semester without hanging yourselves."

With a last withering look at Teddy, she pushed past them and continued on her way.

Teddy's face was red and her jaw was tight, but she didn't say anything until they were halfway down the stairs. Then she muttered, "The nerve of her. What a— *witch!*"

"Teddy, she seemed to be talking directly to you," Iris said. "You've never met her before?"

"Thankfully, I can say no to that!"

"This happens all the time," Beatrice said to Iris. "Back at our old school, lots of girls were jealous of Teddy—because she's so pretty."

"I'd rather be smart," Teddy wailed. "I *am* smart! So why am I *here*, and not at Honoria Wagstaffe?"

When they didn't find Ollie and Cyrus out front, the girls headed around the side of the building. The sun had slipped behind the trees and a cold wind was blowing. Beatrice tightened the wool scarf around her neck and Cayenne stepped gingerly to avoid patches of snow.

"Maybe they've gone back inside," Beatrice said. "It'll be dark soon."

"No, there they are," Teddy said suddenly, "down by the woods."

Beatrice took off toward the boys, with Teddy and Iris hurrying after her. But then, without warning, a deep voice roared from the sky, "Do not enter the woods! I repeat. *Do not enter the woods!*"

Beatrice's eyes jerked in the direction of the voice, but all she could see were some tiny, gauzy creatures buzzing around overhead. It was the sky dancers.

"The woods are off limits from sunset to dawn!" sounded that thunderous voice again, and Beatrice realized with a shock that it was coming from one of the fairies.

"It's okay!" Ollie called out. "The same thing happened to us. Once we stopped, the—um—*guards* backed off."

But even after the girls had reached Ollie and Cyrus, a few feet away from the woods, the sky dancers kept circling and peering down at them.

"What do they *want?*" Teddy muttered.

"We aren't supposed to leave school grounds after the sun goes down," Ollie said, "so I guess they don't want us hiding out in the woods and then sneaking off campus."

"Like we're just dying to prowl around in the woods after dark," Teddy said. "And what could they actually do if we did leave?"

"Forget the sky dancers," Beatrice said abruptly. "There's some stuff we need to talk about."

After introducing Iris to Ollie and Cyrus, she started telling them about the Bane Project, and how Kick had gone with Axel to the headmaster's office in search of the assignments list, after warning him that the project was dangerous.

"What he actually said was, 'Do you really want to work on the Bane Project—and get yourself killed?'"

Ollie raised an eyebrow and Teddy whispered, "*Whoa!*"

"But Axel seemed to think that Kick would be assigned to the project," Beatrice went on. "He said Kick was Cadwallader's pet—since somebody named Milo went away. Oh—and while they were in Cadwallader's office, Axel said something like, 'Maybe you've fooled everyone else, but I know what you're really up to.'"

"And *then*," Teddy added dramatically, "when Beatrice went to her room to get her jacket, guess who was there going through her dresser."

"Kick?" Ollie asked.

"You got it," Teddy said.

"He doesn't *look* like a thief," Iris mused.

"Is there a special thief look I don't know about?" Teddy asked with a grin. "Anyway, whatever he was doing, it's certainly suspicious."

"But back to the Bane Project," Beatrice said. "Axel seems to think that Kick is just as interested in it as he is—for some mysterious reason that Kick won't admit to."

"But Kick told us he doesn't even want to be here," Ollie said, "so why would he *care* about a school project?"

Beatrice nodded. "That's what I'm wondering. Especially one that could get him killed."

8

Magical Intuition

When Beatrice and her friends arrived at the dining room for dinner, they saw that it was just as dark and uninviting as the rest of Widdershins. In the center was a cluster of small tables, each lit by a candle, and at the far end was the faculty table. The rest of the enormous room was swallowed up in shadow. Beatrice noticed Diantha and Axel sitting with a few of the older students, but most of the tables were empty.

Kick was at a table by himself and waved, seeming anxious for them to join him. But just then, a man in black robes came through the door where Beatrice and her friends were standing. Beatrice felt his eyes on her even before she turned to look at him.

He was tall and thin, with salt-and-pepper hair clipped close to the skull and a neatly trimmed beard. The dark eyes that were studying her so intently were framed by glasses with heavy black frames. Beatrice thought he looked serious and scholarly, like a professor, but it seemed that she was the subject that held the greatest interest for him at the moment. In fact, his scrutiny of her was so unwavering, and he was so clearly fascinated by whatever he saw in her face, she felt the sudden impulse to step back.

But in the next instant those eyes switched to low beam and his whole face and manner softened as he smiled at her and said, "Welcome to Widdershins." Then his gaze moved on to include the others. "I'm Dr. Cadwallader, the headmaster."

Her mind leaping back to the image of her crouched behind a desk in his office, Beatrice felt her face grow warm. She started to introduce herself, but he cut her off. "I know who you are, Miss Bailiwick. And I know your friends, as well."

He was still smiling—glowing, actually—as he took them all in, and Beatrice thought he seemed genuinely pleased to meet them.

"I'm anxious to talk to all of you," the headmaster continued. "Come to my office after dinner and we'll get acquainted. It's the last door at the end of the hall." Then he seemed to notice Iris for the first time and his smile dimmed. "And you are . . . ?"

"Iris Tinker," she answered softly, and started to blink.

"Ah, yes, Miss Tinker," he said. "You can wait while I talk with Miss Bailiwick and her companions. Then you and I will meet."

"Y-yes, sir," Iris stammered.

"It's most gratifying to have you all here at Widdershins," the headmaster said, although now his eyes were resting squarely on Beatrice's face again. "I'll see you after dinner."

They watched him stride confidently to the faculty table, where Mrs. Harridan and Toogood Mars were already seated with four others. Their teachers, Beatrice assumed. And she saw that Toogood Mars had exchanged his orange parka and purple hat for plain black robes.

"Do you really want to sit with Kick?" Teddy muttered to Beatrice as they approached the table.

"Maybe he's going to tell us what's going on," Beatrice said quietly.

But as soon as they joined Kick, a small, freckle-faced man in a white apron and red cap arrived with their food. A large tray floated through the air behind him and then hovered at his elbow.

"Hi, Caper," Kick said as the man began to take platters from the tray and place them on the table.

"I'm Fidget," the man corrected him, but he didn't seem offended.

"Sorry," Kick said. "I have trouble telling you Cluricauns apart. Oh, I see, Caper's at the faculty table."

As soon as Fidget was gone, Ollie asked, "What's a Cluricaun?"

"Um—a distant relative of the leprechaun, I believe," Kick said.

He cut his eyes at Beatrice, then turned abruptly to her and said in a rush, "Look, I know we got off to a bad start. I shouldn't have been in your room. I'm sorry—really—and you do deserve an explanation. You see, this girl named Sadie Arrowsmith had that room last year and—well, I needed to look for something of hers. But I should have asked you first."

He gave a soft sigh, as if relieved to have that said. But he looked so depressed, Beatrice felt sorry for him, and found herself believing him.

"The girl—Sadie—" Beatrice said, "she isn't here anymore?"

Kick answered with a glum shake of his head, "No. She—didn't come back."

"So what were you looking for?" Beatrice asked. "Maybe I can help find it."

"It's not there," he said, and sighed again. Then, with a faint smile around the table, he added, "Dig in, you guys. Mud worm meat loaf is Zipporah's specialty. And that's thistle salad with beggar tick dressing. Sounds awful, I know, but it's really pretty good."

Deciding to let him off the hook for the moment, Beatrice started filling her plate. After taking a bite of the meat loaf, she smiled and nodded. Everyone else liked it, too, except for Cyrus, who looked slightly ill as he choked it down.

"I don't see how you people can stand this stuff," he muttered.

"Cyrus, there's more to life than burgers and peanut butter sandwiches," Teddy said. "You need to be open to new things."

But Beatrice was barely listening as Teddy urged Cyrus to try the salad because something else had caught her attention. She'd seen Diantha looking their way when they first sat down, and now the girl was openly staring at them—or, more precisely, staring at Ollie. Beatrice wasn't sure why this bothered her. Okay, so Ollie was good-looking and Diantha had probably noticed. But he'd never give the girl a second glance. Would he?

Trying to put Diantha out of her mind, Beatrice turned her gaze to the faculty. A woman about her parents' age, with a tangle of wild hair piled haphazardly on top of her head, was sitting next to Dr. Cadwallader. On the other side of the headmaster was a bald, heavyset man with impressive jowls. And there were two younger witches, a red-haired man who was grinning and talking nonstop, and a plump, attractive woman who was hanging on to his every word.

Then another man came in and headed for the faculty table. Short and round, he was wearing Kelly-green robes that were shockingly bright and a heavy gold medallion on a chain around his neck. When he sat down and started talking, his voice carried across the room.

"Sorry I'm late, Hodge," the newcomer boomed. "Had a meeting that went on longer than expected. Oh, good, Zipporah made her meat loaf."

Everyone at Beatrice's table had turned around to see where that voice was coming from.

Kick said, "That's Rollo Grubbs, the mayor of Arcana. He and Cadwallader are friends."

Mr. Grubbs, meanwhile, had started shoveling in the food and was still talking while he smacked and chewed.

Noticing how Mrs. Harridan was making a point of not looking at him, and had her nose in the air like she smelled something bad, Beatrice said, "Mrs. H doesn't seem to like the mayor."

"He's a little too loud and uncultured for her taste," Kick said drily. "You can't see it from here, but he wears this humongous diamond ring. And those robes? Dull compared to the rest of his wardrobe."

"Does that woman approve of anyone?" Teddy muttered.

"Just the headmaster," Kick replied, his eyes lingering on the faculty table. "She and Toogood Mars fawn all over him. As far as they're concerned, he can do no wrong."

There was just enough of an edge to his voice to make Beatrice ask, "And what do you think?"

His eyes met hers for a split second and then he lowered his head over his plate. "That's not for me to say," he answered, and took another bite of meat loaf.

Fidget had just brought the centipede pudding for dessert when Beatrice noticed that her plate was moving, ever so slowly, toward the edge of the table. Then she realized that the table itself was vibrating, as was her chair.

"I think the monster's awake," she said.

"Aw, man," Kick muttered, "not again."

Now they could hear raised voices at other tables.

"—floor's shaking, too."

"—must be welcoming us back."

"But twice in one day? *That's* never happened before."

"So the monster's more active today than normal?" Beatrice asked Kick.

"Oh, yeah. Usually we only get a good shaking once or twice a month."

But by the time they'd had a few bites of pudding, the vibrations had stopped and Kick said, "Good. That was a mild one. A few times, late at night, I've felt the building shake so hard, I thought it was going to collapse. It even threw me out of bed once. And when that happens, you know the thing's come aboveground, stomping around, and the next day you'll hear that people are missing. But these little tremors are nothing to worry about."

After dinner, they ran into Diantha as they left the dining room. Beatrice was pretty sure this wasn't a coincidence, especially when Diantha made an embarrassing fuss over Ollie as she introduced herself—and pointedly ignored the rest of them. Of course, being a gentleman, Ollie was polite, while Beatrice tried hard to keep a pleasant expression on her face. But behind Diantha's back, Teddy was pretending to gag.

When they finally got away from Diantha, Kick said, "Well, let me know how your meeting with Cadwallader goes. I'll be interested in what he has to say."

The words were spoken casually enough, but, again, Beatrice picked up on something in Kick's voice that made her wonder.

Toogood Mars was sitting behind the desk where Beatrice had hidden earlier that day. When she and her friends walked in, he glanced up from the papers he was holding and said, "Take a seat. Dr. Cadwallader will be with you shortly," and went back to his reading.

They sat down in chairs against the wall and waited. With Toogood there, it was impossible to discuss anything that mattered, so they didn't talk at all. The only sound in the room was the rustle of paper as Toogood turned a page.

It had been a long day, and Beatrice was tired. Her eyelids were beginning to droop and she was fighting to hold back a yawn when all of a sudden a burst of sound like the blare of a trumpet filled the small room. Teddy shrieked and Iris cowered, while the rest of them leaped to their feet.

But Toogood Mars hadn't so much as flinched. He just stared at them as if they'd lost their minds. Then he said, "Dr. Cadwallader will see you now," and pointed to the closed door behind him.

Leaving Iris still huddled and blinking in her chair, the other four made a shaky entrance into the headmaster's office.

It was small and dimly lit, the stone walls lined with bookshelves that sagged under the weight of dusty, leather-bound volumes that looked as if they hadn't been touched in a century. More books were stacked on top of the desk, along with a burned-down candle that provided the only light in the room and—a trumpet. The only other item of interest was a sword hanging on the wall behind the headmaster's desk, its long blade gleaming in the flickering light. And, of course, there was the headmaster, himself, sitting at the desk and watching them as they came through the door.

"Pull those chairs over," Dr. Cadwallader directed.

Once they were seated in front of his desk, the headmaster said, "I should start by telling you that I'm fully aware of Widdershins' undesirable reputation—and I don't mind a bit. In fact, I encourage it because it's that reputation that keeps people away, allowing us to pursue our work undisturbed.

How strange, Beatrice thought. *He* wants *Widdershins to be known as a school for losers.*

"I've been doing research in a particular field since my university days," Dr. Cadwallader went on, "and when I was offered the position of headmaster at Widdershins four years ago, I accepted immediately. Do you know why? Because I liked the idea of involving students in my work. Of course, that meant selecting just the right students to come here."

Beatrice's heart was beating fast. She was anxious to learn why she and her friends had been brought to Widdershins, but, at the same time, she was almost afraid to hear what the headmaster was about to say.

"It's a tricky business, choosing just the right ones," Dr. Cadwallader continued. "Unlike my colleagues, I go through every application that comes into the Department of Witch Education."

The headmaster had leaned forward and was looking intently at Beatrice, just as he had in the dining room. For some reason, it made the hair stand up on the back of her neck.

"I look for traits and life experiences in my students that other headmasters and headmistresses dismiss as insignificant," he went on quietly, his eyes not moving from her face. "Because they're in search of the student who can cast the most flamboyant spell or brew the most complicated potion, but I don't care about that. What I'm looking for is a very special quality that I've come to call"—he paused for dramatic effect and then finished with a sweep of his hand—"*magical intuition.*"

Of course, Beatrice and the others didn't know what he was talking about. And as his lips curved into a half smile, Beatrice realized that he enjoyed keeping them in the dark. It made him feel powerful. And that was when it dawned on her that she didn't like the man very much.

"The theory of magical intuition," Dr. Cadwallader said, regarding them smugly as he leaned back in his chair, "is mine and mine alone. Back in my student days, I was working with test subjects who had been through some type of traumatic event—a serious accident on a broom, a close encounter with a ghoul, something of that sort—and as I worked with them, I noticed a strange phenomenon. Most of the subjects had no particular talent for traditional magic, and yet, each had escaped a potentially fatal experience with little, or no, physical injury. When choosing between different courses of action in a dangerous situation, they had seemed to know intuitively the best course to take. Even when logic pointed them in another direction."

Dr. Cadwallader was no longer smiling, but Beatrice saw the excitement in his eyes, how they glittered in the candlelight.

"In their talks with me," the headmaster continued, "they even used the word *know* repeatedly. *I seemed to know that I shouldn't take the direct route, even though it was shorter,* one of them said. Or, *Somehow I knew that goblin would be waiting on the other side of the door.* And that," Dr. Cadwallader said, "is how I began my life's work: the study of individuals who instinctively know things that defy logical explanation."

"You mean, like ESP," Ollie said.

"No!" Dr. Cadwallader sat straight up in his chair in vehement protest. "No, no, no—*That* is a mortal concept. Magical intuition is something else entirely, something that only witches—and a small percentage of those—will ever experience. I've written papers on different aspects of my research," he said, looking moody now, maybe even a little angry, "but no one in the academic community recognizes what a groundbreaking discovery this is. As I mentioned earlier, it's the flamboyant frippery that impresses most people. But I know I'm on to something. I've seen it over and over—witches who have the instinct, who *know* how to proceed in order to avoid catastrophe. Witches who have magical intuition."

"And you think we have it?" Beatrice asked doubtfully.

"Oh, yes," the headmaster said. "The four of you

most certainly have it. I've followed your exploits with Dally Rumpe. I've read your files a dozen times. And this is what I see: You have virtually no ability in traditional magic, and yet, you were able to make choices that allowed you to survive life-and-death battles with a powerful sorcerer. And *defeat* him! Oh, you have no idea how exciting this is for me!" he said, his face glowing. "To have four young witches with such obvious talent—who are used to working together, already a team—as students in my school! You four are going to help me prove my theory. Together, we'll make my detractors eat their words!"

Beatrice tried to keep her expression neutral, hoping he couldn't see in her face what she was feeling: a growing dislike and distrust—and was there just a sliver of fear mixed in? Because of the wild gleam in his eyes? Because, at that moment, he seemed just a little bit nuts?

"But how can we help?" Teddy asked. "What do we have to do?"

"You'll begin with intensive study in magical intuition," the headmaster said. "And when you're ready, you'll start your fieldwork."

The fieldwork that might kill us, Beatrice thought.

"What is the fieldwork exactly?" Ollie asked.

"Students at Widdershins have individual semester projects," Dr. Cadwallader replied, "where they apply what they've learned in the classroom. Unfortunately," he added with a scowl, "most students have had insignificant projects because they haven't shown the talent necessary for anything important. But there's a special assignment I've been planning for a long time. I've just been waiting for the right students."

His eyes glittered feverishly as they came to rest on Beatrice again. "And now," he said softly, I have them."

9

The Mad Doctor

Beatrice was beginning to understand. The headmaster was just using them to prove himself to those academic bigwigs. And that secret project of his? It had to be the Bane Project.

"Could you tell us more about this special assignment?" she asked.

"No," Dr. Cadwallader said curtly. "You aren't ready to hear about it yet."

Teddy had that determined look on her face. She was always ready to push the limits, regardless of the consequences.

"Is it by any chance," she asked, "the Bane Project?"

Dr. Cadwallader's jaw dropped and he just stared at her. Beatrice took a quick breath, amazed by Teddy's daring. But they had both guessed right! It was written all over his face.

The headmaster had gone rigid with fury and now he burst out, "Who told you about the Bane Project?"

"Um—no one," Teddy said, appearing less sure of herself now. "I don't have any idea what it is."

"But you've heard talk about it."

He was so agitated, Teddy was looking like she wished she'd never brought it up. "Someone mentioned the name," she mumbled, "that's all."

The headmaster's eyes were still burning into Teddy's face. Then he looked away and seemed to study the books on his desk for a long time before turning back to them. Only his tightly clenched jaw betrayed the emotion he was still struggling to control.

"The Bane Project," he said carefully, "is none of your concern at the moment. So let's talk about things you *do* need to know. You may leave campus after classes have ended for the day, as long as you sign out and take at least two other people with you. But you must be back by sunset. No excuses for being late will be accepted."

He had reached for the trumpet and was turning it over and over in his hands, not bothering to look at them as he spoke. Clearly, he was still angry.

"I'm sure you've heard about Arcana's monster," he went on, "and felt it move a couple of times today. But you'll be perfectly safe as long as you follow the rules. There's a student lounge next to the dining room. Feel free to use it, but all students must be in their own rooms with lights out by ten. Do you have any questions?"

He finally looked up as they all murmured, "No, sir."

"Very well," he said gruffly. "Before you go, I have one last thing to tell you. Rumors are an unavoidable part of life in a witch academy, and the vast majority are untrue. So I trust you won't believe everything you hear. The Widdershins' grapevine is notoriously unreliable."

Then he smiled, a stiff, practiced lifting of his lips without a trace of warmth, and said, "You're dismissed."

Iris was still waiting outside, blinking and quivering and looking like she might faint. Beatrice leaned down and whispered in her ear, "Nothing to worry about. Come to my room when you're finished."

After they'd left the headmaster's office, Beatrice said, "What do you guys think about this magical intuition?"

"There could be something to it," Ollie replied. "Cadwallader didn't like it when I compared magical intuition to ESP, but they sound similar, don't they? I guess he just wants to think he's being totally original."

"But do you think we have that sort of intuition?" Beatrice asked. "Did we break Dally Rumpe's spell and get out alive because we somehow *knew* what to do? At the time, it seemed more like dumb luck to me."

"But it *would* explain a lot," Ollie mused. "How we were able to do it all with such limited magic."

"I guess." Beatrice frowned. "But whether he's right about that or not, I think all Cadwallader cares about is showing the world how brilliant he is, even if it means putting his students' lives at risk. I'm beginning to feel like a lab rat—at the mercy of the mad doctor."

"And why wouldn't he tell us about the Bane Project?" Teddy demanded. "That has to be what he's planning for us."

"Well, if it *is* dangerous," Beatrice said, "maybe he was afraid of scaring us off."

They had passed the dining room when Ollie stopped at a darkened doorway and said, "This must be the student lounge."

He stepped inside and turned on the light. It didn't surprise anyone that the room was gloomy and filled with shadows. There were a few bookshelves and a stack of magazines on a table, but no television, no DVDs, no music. And the lumpy chairs and couches looked about as comfortable as the beds upstairs.

Beatrice was scanning book titles when Teddy said, "Now that we've met with Cadwallader, maybe we can get Kick to tell us what he knows about the Bane Project. He did open up a little at dinner. Why don't you go upstairs and get him, Ollie? We'll wait for you here."

Cyrus hadn't opened his mouth all evening, but now he said in a listless voice, "I'm kind of tired. I think I'll go to bed."

Beatrice turned around to tell him that it wasn't even eight o'clock yet, but stopped herself when she saw how pale and weary he looked. Could he be sick? Or maybe it was just the stress of coming here.

Hoping that a good night's sleep was all he needed, Beatrice said, "We're all tired. Why don't we wait till tomorrow to talk to Kick?"

Teddy started to protest, but Ollie said, "That sounds good to me. It's been a long day."

They said good night on the third-floor landing, then Beatrice and Teddy went to Beatrice's room to wait for Iris. It wasn't long before there was a tap on the door and Iris popped her head in. She was actually smiling as she bounced into the room and took a seat next to Teddy on the end of Beatrice's bed.

Then she said in a voice that could only be described as bubbly, "For as long as I can remember, I've known things that other people don't. And now I understand why."

"Magical intuition?" Beatrice asked.

"*Exactly*," Iris said. "Dr. Cadwallader reminded me of when my mother was in a car accident and the doctors said they were going to have to amputate one of her legs. I was only eight at the time and didn't know much about healing, but, *somehow*, I knew she didn't need the surgery. And since she'd come to rely on my instincts, she told them not to operate and her leg healed on its own."

"Wow," Beatrice said. "Maybe there is something to this magical intuition stuff."

"You just don't know how much it means to me," Iris said softly, "to be told that I'm—special. I never fit in at my old school. Kids seemed to sense that there was something peculiar about me."

"Welcome to our world," Teddy said cheerfully.

"Anyway, I was afraid it wouldn't be any different here," Iris went on, "because I didn't have formal training in magic. So I started reading everything I could get my hands on, trying to learn as much as possible before classes started. Only that just made me realize even more how little I knew. Then I met the two of you, and Ollie and Cyrus, and you were all so nice, I started to feel better, not so alone. And now Dr. Cadwallader says he expects great things from me. . . ." She shook her head in wonder. "It's just more than I'd ever imagined. And he even said he might assign me to a big project he has planned. Did he mention that to you?"

Beatrice nodded. "He said we might be working on it, too."

Iris clapped her hands and bounced up and down on the bed. "Then it's even better than I thought! Won't this be fun, all of us together? You know, it's just like Kick said: We aren't here because we're losers; we were *chosen*."

It was so cold in her room, Beatrice put on a sweater over her flannel pajamas before hopping into bed. The mattress was hard and the pillow was flat, but snuggling under two blankets, with Cayenne curled up against her neck, she finally got warm.

Even so, there were so many thoughts swirling around inside her head, she couldn't go to sleep. She wondered what Kick had been looking for in her room. And what secret he was keeping that Axel had guessed. It was something more dangerous than the Bane Project, Axel had said. And just what *was* the Bane Project, anyway?

It was hours later when Beatrice woke with a start to a clanging sound outside her room, followed by moans and then a shriek that sent chills up her spine.

Cayenne had slipped out from under the covers and was staring at the door, growling softly.

Beatrice crawled out of bed and shoved her feet into her icy dragon slippers. When she opened the door, she saw a dark figure with long hair shuffling down the hall, wailing and groaning and beating a cooking pot with a spoon. Beatrice sighed and closed her door again. It was just Rhude, pretending—badly—to be a ghost.

Beatrice ran back to bed and burrowed under the covers. A while later, after the dark-side fairy had left to haunt some other corridor and Beatrice's teeth had finally stopped chattering, she thought she might be able to go back to sleep. But just then, there was a knock on the door.

This time Beatrice sprang out of bed, prepared to tell Rhude to get lost. But when she jerked open the door, it was Ollie standing there. Light from the candle he was holding flickered across his face and Beatrice could see that he looked anxious—maybe even scared.

"What's wrong?" she asked quickly.

"It's Cyrus," Ollie whispered. "He's having some kind of—spell. I think you'd better come."

Beatrice grabbed for her robe and slippers. "I'll get Teddy," she said. "And Iris, too. She knows about healing."

Minutes later, the four of them were racing up the stairs and then down the fourth-floor corridor. Ollie threw open the door to Cyrus's room and ran inside, with Teddy and Iris on his heels. But Beatrice stopped short at the threshold, stunned by what she saw.

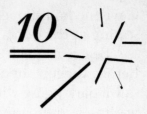

In Crisis

S tanding at the end of his bed, Cyrus was rocking gently from side to side. His eyes were rolled back in his head and he was moaning softly.

"I heard him yell," Ollie said, "and when I came in to see what was wrong, I found him—like this. I thought he must be dreaming, so I tried to wake him, but I couldn't. He just started to make that noise and then he muttered something I couldn't understand."

Beatrice came slowly into the room, her eyes fixed on Cyrus's swaying body. "Iris," she said, "have you ever seen anything like this?"

Iris was studying Cyrus's face. "I've never witnessed it myself," she said quietly, "but I've read about it. I think he's in a trance."

Teddy let out a gasp. "You mean, he's been enchanted?"

"Maybe," Iris answered. "Trances can be caused by enchantments or potions—or emotional trauma. I can't tell what's causing this."

"Well, can you fix it?" Teddy asked urgently.

"Listen." Ollie held up his hand. "He's saying something."

The words coming out of Cyrus's mouth were spoken so softly Beatrice had to strain to hear. She thought he was saying *fire*, and maybe *flames*, over and over. Then, without warning, he started to shake his head violently.

"Burning," he screamed. "All of it—burning!"

After that, he grew quiet and started rocking again.

Iris was still looking intently into Cyrus's face. "He seemed terrified when he cried out, like he was actually *experiencing* some frightening event. I think he might be reliving something that happened to him."

"A fire?" Beatrice looked at Teddy and Ollie. "Do either of you remember any fires at the Rascallion house?"

Ollie and Teddy shook their heads no.

Then all of a sudden Cyrus started shouting in a panicked voice, "It's falling down! *Crash! Boom!*"

Unnerved, Beatrice said, "Iris, what can we do?"

"If I'm right," Iris answered, "and he really is reliving something from his past, I might be able to bring him out of it."

"Then try," Beatrice said, "please."

Iris placed her hands on Cyrus's head. Then she closed her eyes and started swaying with him, a look of absolute concentration on her face.

Watching them, Beatrice wondered how this could be happening. It was like a bad dream. And Cyrus, of all people. He'd always been healthy—and happy. What could be causing this?

Then Beatrice had the fleeting thought that maybe they should wake Toogood Mars or Mrs. Harridan.

What if Cyrus needed to go to a hospital? But she shied away from that idea immediately. It was different here. Who knew what they might do to him in a witch hospital?

That was when she realized, thankfully, that Cyrus's rocking had begun to slow down. Then his eyes rolled back to where they were supposed to be and he was still.

"He's coming out of it," Teddy whispered.

Ollie touched Cyrus's shoulder. "You're going to be okay," he said softly.

Iris opened her eyes and looked steadily at Cyrus, whose gaze was drifting lazily around the room.

"What happened?" Cyrus asked, appearing groggy. "Why are you all here?"

"I heard you call out," Ollie said. "I thought you were having a nightmare."

Cyrus yawned and started toward the bed, weaving a little. He crawled in under the covers and closed his eyes. "I don't have nightmares," he mumbled. And then he went to sleep.

"Iris, thank you," Beatrice whispered.

"That was *terrible*," Teddy said. "Is he all right?"

"He'll sleep now," Iris said, "but there's no telling when he might have another one."

"It could happen again?" Teddy looked horrified.

Nodding, Iris said, "Someone should stay with him."

"I'll stay," Ollie said.

"You most certainly will not!"

They all turned toward the voice and saw Mrs. Harridan standing in the doorway. Behind her were

Toogood Mars and Diantha. In that instant when their eyes met, Beatrice saw that Diantha was looking blatantly smug.

"If this boy is sick, he needs medical professionals caring for him, not children," Mrs. Harridan said. She marched into the room, wearing a pink quilted robe and carrying a candle. Her hair was down, hanging over her shoulder in a long braid.

"He isn't sick," Beatrice said quickly. "He just had a nightmare."

"I saw enough to know that wasn't any ordinary nightmare," Mrs. Harridan said, frowning as she stared down at Cyrus. "This boy is in crisis. Obviously, he's deeply disturbed."

"He isn't—*disturbed!*" Beatrice said indignantly. "He's just . . ." But she didn't finish because she wasn't sure *what* Cyrus was.

"And why are you in the boys' dorm?" Mrs. Harridan asked Beatrice in a cold voice. Her eyes shifted to Teddy, then Iris, who cringed and started to blink. "I believe I told you the rules this afternoon. But you thought I'd never know. And I might not have if Miss Winter-Rose hadn't come to tell me that you left your room with a *boy*, Miss Bailiwick."

Beatrice cut her eyes at Diantha, who was looking pleased with herself.

"Toogood," Mrs. Harridan said abruptly, "you'd better stay in here tonight. We'll meet with Dr. Cadwallader in the morning and decide what to do. As for the rest of you, back to your beds. I'll be patrolling the halls, and I'd better not see you leave your rooms until breakfast."

"But if Cyrus wakes up, he'll feel better if one of us is here," Ollie said. "Couldn't I—"

"What did I say?" Mrs. Harridan snapped. "Go to bed, Mr. Tibbs."

Beatrice looked at Cyrus, who was now sleeping peacefully, unaware of the drama going on around him. She agreed with Ollie; one of Cyrus's friends should stay with him, *not* Toogood Mars. But knowing that they'd never change Mrs. Harridan's mind, Beatrice followed Teddy and Iris from the room.

Diantha was walking behind them as they started down the hall and Teddy whipped around to face her. "I can't believe you snitched! Our friend needed us. But I guess you'd have to *have* friends to understand that."

Diantha looked momentarily taken aback, but then that satisfied smirk reappeared and she said, "All of you think you're above the rules just because you've had your names in the paper. But *I* don't see anything special about any of you. And if I were *you*," she added, looking hard at Beatrice, "I wouldn't try sneaking out with my boyfriend again. Not unless you're just dying to be expelled."

"Save the advice," Teddy snarled. "We don't need it."

Diantha gave her a withering look and headed for the stairs, looking disgustingly stylish in her white silk robe and slippers.

Teddy was muttering under her breath all the way to the third floor, but Beatrice was pensive, thinking about

Diantha and why she was so nasty to them. Obviously, she'd seen the articles and photos like everyone else, and for some people, that was reason enough to be jealous. And that dig about Beatrice's boyfriend had been telling. Diantha *did* like Ollie—or, at least, she wanted his undivided attention.

Once in bed, Beatrice snuggled up with Cayenne and closed her eyes. But her mind was spinning and sleep wouldn't come. She was thinking about Cyrus and all the scary things he'd been doing and saying. She kept seeing him with his eyes rolled back in his head, and hearing Mrs. Harridan's words. *This boy is in crisis.*

11

The Enchantment

T he next morning, everyone tried to be cheerful for Cyrus's sake. Ollie had pulled Beatrice
aside before they went into breakfast to tell
her that Cyrus didn't remember much about the night
before, just what he thought were bad dreams.

"But Toogood Mars couldn't wait to fill him in,"
Ollie had told her in disgust. "And you should have
seen Cyrus's face when he heard everything that happened. He was in total shock. Anyway, he has a meeting with Cadwallader after breakfast, and I asked if I
could go with him, but Toogood wouldn't let me."

For breakfast, Fidget brought them scrambled serpent's eggs, sage toast with damselfly jelly, and bowls of
cereal with dragon's milk and fruit flies. After a sleepless
night, Beatrice wasn't especially hungry, which turned
out to be just as well. Because when she looked down at
her plate, she saw that her eggs had globs of red in
them—like clots of blood. And the cereal! Instead of
oatmeal, her bowl was filled with a mound of white,
crawly things that *moved*. On closer inspection, Beatrice
decided they were maggots.

"Oh, *yuck!*" she exclaimed, and shoved the bowl away.

"What's wrong?" Teddy asked, and then saw for herself and looked sick. "*Maggots? Is that what those are?*"

"My food looks fine," Ollie said, glancing around at the other plates and bowls. "Everyone's does—except yours, Beatrice."

"Well, even Zipporah doesn't get *this* creative," Kick said, and called Fidget back over to the table.

"Look at this," Kick said to the waiter, pointing at Beatrice's breakfast.

Fidget looked, then shrugged. "Hey, I just bring it out here. You want more eggs and cereal?" he asked Beatrice.

Having lost her appetite completely, Beatrice said, "I think I'll pass. Just take this away, okay?"

After Fidget had left with Beatrice's dishes, Cyrus said, "That wasn't much worse than *regular* witch food."

"It was disgusting," Teddy said, wrinkling her forehead and her nose. "We should complain about the cooking in this place."

"Zipporah wouldn't have served something like that," Kick said firmly. "She takes pride in feeding us well. Someone must have tampered with your food, Beatrice."

"But who?" she asked. "And why?"

Kick shook his head. "I don't know. Maybe someone here doesn't like you."

"Well, there's Diantha," Beatrice said. "And I don't think Mrs. Harridan is too fond of me, either. But I can't

103

see her putting *maggots* in my cereal bowl." Beatrice shuddered.

"Wait," Ollie said suddenly. "Maybe this is tied in with those guys on the bus. Maybe they *were* after you, Beatrice."

"But kidnapping is serious," Beatrice said, "and this breakfast thing—as gross as it is—seems more like a prank."

"If someone wants you out of here," Kick said thoughtfully, "they might try anything and everything to see what works."

"Kick's right," Ollie said, looking worried. "You may not be safe, Beatrice. We should've told someone about the attack on the bus."

"I was going to mention it when we met with Cadwallader," Beatrice said, "but I got the feeling he wouldn't have cared."

Ollie nodded and Kick said, "Not unless he thought it would make *him* look bad."

Iris slid a plate of toast toward Beatrice. "Here. You have to eat something."

Beatrice took a piece of toast and nibbled on it half-heartedly as she glanced around the room. There were some new faces this morning and fewer empty chairs. The sound of conversation made the dining room seem almost pleasant. But then Beatrice saw Diantha looking their way, with her signature smirk, and that sort of ruined the moment.

As they left the dining room, they stayed close to Cyrus, wanting to give him moral support.

"When Cadwallader asks you what happened last night," Teddy told him, "just say you had a nightmare."

"But . . . I don't think it was," Cyrus said, looking troubled. "I've been going over it in my mind and it all seemed so—*real*."

Beatrice wondered what Cyrus had remembered about the previous night, but she didn't want to upset him, so all she said was, "Nightmares always seem real. You were just tired and in a strange place. Dr. Cadwallader will understand that."

Teddy shot her a look that said, *Oh, sure he will.*

"We'll wait for you in the lounge," Ollie said to Cyrus. "And don't worry. Everything's going to be fine."

Cyrus started toward the headmaster's office with his head down and shoulders slumped, looking like he didn't expect anything good to come out of this. The rest of them went into the lounge to wait.

Kick flopped down on a couch and dust billowed out.

"I know it's none of my business," he said, "but what exactly happened to Cyrus last night?"

Ollie told him quickly about the trance and Mrs. Harridan showing up at the worst possible moment.

"Thanks to the delightful Diantha," Teddy added, scowling. "What a pain in the neck!"

Kick nodded solemnly. "I'll have to tell you about Diantha sometime."

"There's lots you may be able to tell us," Beatrice said quickly. "We met with Cadwallader, and he told us about his magical intuition theory—"

"Not now," Kick said abruptly, glancing nervously toward the door. "You never know who might be listening. We'll talk later."

Iris found a book titled *The Last of the Banshees* and curled up in a chair to read. Kick flipped through an ancient copy of *Enchantment News*. But Beatrice, Teddy, and Ollie were too worried to do anything except pace.

It seemed like Cyrus was gone for a long time. And when he finally came through the door, Beatrice took one look at his strained face and knew he wasn't bringing good news.

"I blew it," Cyrus said bluntly.

"Tell us what happened," Teddy said.

"Well, Dr. Cadwallader and Mrs. Harridan started firing questions at me," Cyrus said, "like they were the police and I was a criminal, and I just kept saying that I'd had a nightmare, but Mrs. Harridan said it was more than that and, I don't know, they kept on and on and— it just all came spilling out!"

Tears sprang to his eyes and Beatrice put her arm around his shoulders. "It's okay," she said.

"What do you mean, it all came spilling out?" Teddy asked. "What *all*?"

Cyrus sniffed and wiped at his eyes with the back of his hand. "I didn't want you to know . . . I thought . . . I thought I could handle it on my own, but . . . but it just keeps getting worse!"

"Tell us what's going on," Ollie said gently.

Cyrus nodded and took a shaky breath. "Well, it started at home. I just had this terrible feeling about coming back to the Sphere. Dreading it, you know?

And after we learned we were coming to Widdershins, I started having bad dreams—only now I think they've been happening when I was awake, too—sort of like visions. I—I told Dr. Cadwallader and Mrs. Harridan that I couldn't remember them, but that was only partly true."

He sat down heavily on the couch next to Kick.

"You mean, you do remember the dreams?" Beatrice asked.

"Just little bits," Cyrus mumbled. "I saw . . . walls caving in and buildings on fire." He shivered. "And people were . . . running and screaming."

Teddy crouched down beside him. "Did you recognize anyone?"

Cyrus shook his head. "I couldn't see faces, and I don't know what they were running from, but it's the same scene every time, the same walls crashing down and bricks flying and flames everywhere. And since we've been here," he went on wearily, "the visions have seemed *more* real. I didn't tell any of you about them because it was all so strange. I thought maybe I was losing my mind."

"Oh, Cyrus," Beatrice said, dropping to the floor beside Teddy and taking his hand, "you can tell us anything."

Cyrus looked at her sadly. "No, Beatrice, I can't. Because I won't be seeing you anymore. Dr. Cadwallader thinks I'm—what did he say?—*too unstable* to be here. So he's sending me home. Today."

Beatrice was too stunned to speak. It was Teddy who said, "*What?* Yesterday he couldn't say enough good things about us and now he's sending one of us home. Because of a nightmare. Or a vision, or whatever it is. Well, we'll just have to go talk to him. Right, Beatrice? Ollie?"

"Wait, Teddy," Cyrus said. "I don't want to leave you guys, but I guess I never should have come here in the first place. It's just—you know how sometimes you have a feeling that you're *meant* to do something, whether you want to or not? Well, that's how I felt about coming to Widdershins. Like there's something I'm supposed to do here." He sighed. "But I think I'm ready to go home."

When they went upstairs to help him pack, Beatrice didn't care if she was breaking the rules or not. She was sad about Cyrus leaving, but at the same time, she wondered if this might not be the best thing. Because there was definitely something about this place that Cyrus couldn't handle.

By the time they arrived downstairs with his trunk, Toogood Mars had pulled the old *Happy Hills* bus up to the front door.

"I envy you getting out of here," Teddy said to Cyrus.

"Write to us," Beatrice said. "Promise?"

Then everyone was hugging him and telling him to take care of himself, while Toogood Mars—once again in his orange parka and purple hat—loaded the trunk on the bus. They watched Cyrus climb the steps and take a seat, and everyone waved as the bus took off down the driveway. They kept waving until it was out of sight.

"You know," Beatrice said glumly to Ollie as they went back inside, "I almost wish I were on that bus with him."

Then they saw Mrs. Harridan standing at the bottom of the stairs, obviously waiting for them and more than a little impatient.

"Yeah, I know what you mean," Ollie muttered.

The dorm matron was passing out class schedules. Most of the students had already gotten theirs and were wandering off talking about them when Mrs. Harridan thrust Beatrice's schedule at her. It turned out that she, Ollie, Teddy, and Iris were all down for the same courses.

"Look," Iris said, "we have Dr. Cadwallader for Independent Study and Fieldwork in the afternoons."

"The big man himself," Teddy said sarcastically.

Beatrice was feeling down about Cyrus leaving, and Ollie, always sensitive to her moods, gave her a sympathetic smile. "I know," he said, "I'm going to miss him, too. But since the rest of us are stuck here, we might as well make the best of it. Why don't we find Kick and see if he'll tell us about the Bane Project? I'll go check upstairs."

A few minutes later, Ollie was back, shaking his head. "He wasn't in his room or Axel's, either. Let's look outside."

They trooped out the front door and down the steps—and came to an abrupt halt. Because rattling up the gravel drive was the *Happy Hills* bus. And Cyrus was inside, waving to them.

As soon as Toogood Mars had parked and opened the door, Cyrus came barreling down the steps.

"What in the world?" Teddy muttered.

"You aren't going to believe this," Cyrus said breathlessly. "It's really bad!"

"Tell us," Ollie said.

"Well, we went through Arcana," Cyrus said, "and we came to the city limits and then—the bus stalled."

"No big surprise," Beatrice said. "Just look at it!"

"So Toogood Mars got out and fiddled with something under the hood," Cyrus went on, "several times, but it still wouldn't start. Then I got out to see what he was doing, and I must've . . . I guess I had to have—"

"Come on," Teddy said, "spit it out."

Cyrus gulped in some air and said, "I must've stepped outside the city limits. Because—just like that, I was *frozen!* I could see and hear and think—I just couldn't move."

They were all looking at him in astonishment.

"Toogood was staring at me with his eyes bugged out," Cyrus continued, "and he was saying, 'This shouldn't be. Students are immune to the enchantment. It only works on people who were here when the monster put it in place.' But then, after a few minutes, I could move again and Toogood told me to get on the bus, we were going back to Widdershins. And get this— once he decided that, the bus started right up. No problem."

Toogood Mars was hurrying up the front steps, with Cyrus's trunk floating behind him. "You wait in the lounge," he called out to Cyrus. "Dr. C's going to want to talk to you once he figures out what to do."

After Toogood had gone inside, Ollie said to Cyrus, "This doesn't make sense. You *should* have been protected."

"Well, I wasn't," Cyrus said, looking panicky. "So what if I have to stay in Arcana for the rest of my life? This is my *least* favorite part of the Witches' Sphere."

"Mine, too," Teddy said. Then she caught her breath sharply. "I just thought of something. What if *none* of us can ever leave here?"

Beatrice was staring at her. "You're right. If Cyrus isn't protected, we might not be, either."

"We'd better see if anything happens when the rest of us try to leave," Ollie said. "But we need someone who knows the city."

Beatrice and Ollie finally found Kick bouncing a basketball in a dark, enormous room that was designated as the gym. There were no hoops, but occasionally, Kick would leap up and toss the ball into the air like he was aiming at a basket. He waved when he saw Beatrice and Ollie and dribbled his way over to them.

"See why I want to go back home?" he asked cheerfully. "This place doesn't even know what basketball is. Or baseball or football, for that matter." Then he paused, studying Beatrice's face. "So what's up? You need something?"

"A tour guide," Beatrice said.

It was decided that Teddy would stay with Cyrus, while Beatrice, Ollie, and Iris would go into Arcana with Kick. After they'd signed out and started down the driveway, Ollie said, "I'll bet Cyrus is the only one of us affected by the enchantment. It just goes along with all the other strange things happening to him."

"You're probably right," Beatrice said, "but we should make sure."

They were approaching the gates when one of the sky dancers flew past and bellowed into Beatrice's ear, "Be back before sunset! And watch out for Bane!"

Beatrice, Ollie, and Iris exchanged startled looks.

"Did she say *Bane?*" Iris asked.

"That's right," Kick said as they passed through the gates. "They're always telling us to watch out for him when we leave campus."

"Who *is* Bane?" Ollie asked.

Kick looked surprised. "I thought you knew. Bane is what the witches in Arcana call the monster, short for Bane of Our Lives."

Seeing the sudden excitement on Beatrice's face, Kick stared at her. "What?" he asked.

They were out on a city street now and a male witch was walking toward them.

"We'll tell you when we get back to school," Beatrice whispered.

"Okay," Kick said, "then let's get going."

He led them through a maze of streets that were just as bleak and dirty as Beatrice remembered. Finally, he stopped at a corner and said, "See that yellow line on the pavement up ahead? That's where the city limits end."

The four walked up to the line and looked down at it.

"So who wants to go first?" Beatrice asked.

"I will," Ollie said. "The rest of you wait and see what happens to me."

He stepped across the line and nothing happened. The enchantment didn't affect him. Then Beatrice, Iris, and Kick tried, with the same results.

Beatrice blew her bangs out of her eyes and stared hard at the yellow line. "I don't get this," she said. "Why are we protected and Cyrus isn't? What's so different about him?"

12

Kick's Secret

The dining room was noisy when Beatrice, Ollie, and Kick rushed in for lunch, with most of the tables filled. Teddy waved them over to a table on the far side, where she was sitting with Cyrus.

"So?" Cyrus prompted as Beatrice slipped into a chair beside him.

"Nothing happened," Beatrice said. "We weren't frozen."

Cyrus managed a weak smile. "Well, I'm glad all of you aren't stuck here, anyway."

"I could be," Teddy said, but she didn't seem worried. It was pretty clear that Cyrus was the only one of them who was a captive in Arcana.

Fidget arrived with their food—slugs and boiled skunk cabbage that looked so slippery, no one was especially eager to dig in—and Beatrice inspected hers carefully before taking a tentative bite.

"Zipporah's one failure," Kick said. "But at least yours doesn't look any worse than ours, Beatrice."

While cutting a giant slug into small pieces for Cayenne, Beatrice glanced at Cyrus and said, "Did you see Dr. Cadwallader?"

Cyrus nodded and sighed. "He acted like I'd frozen myself on purpose—just to make his day. He looked at me through those big glasses and said, 'Until the matter of you not being able to leave is resolved, young man, I suppose you'll *have* to stay here with us.'"

"Brilliant deduction," Teddy muttered.

"But he was glad that he hadn't gotten around to notifying my parents that he was sending me home," Cyrus added. "And he said for me not to write them just yet, that there was no need to worry them."

"*He's* probably the one who's worried," Beatrice said.

"No kidding," Teddy said. "How would it look if word got out that one of his students turned into a Popsicle when he tried to leave the city?"

"Will you be going to class with us?" Ollie asked Cyrus.

"Yeah, Mrs. Harridan gave me my schedule," Cyrus said, "and it's the same as yours. But I'm not allowed to go into Arcana at all. And I have to meet with Mrs. Harridan every day to discuss any *problems* I'm having." Cyrus made a face. "I'm supposed to see her right after lunch. But, you know, even if I am a prisoner here, I'm feeling better. I think it's helped telling you guys about everything. Well . . . *almost* everything."

Beatrice gave him a stern look. "You mean you're still holding out on us?"

"There's just one detail I forgot to tell you," Cyrus said hastily. "You know the visions I have of buildings falling down and burning? Well, I'm pretty sure it's happening in Arcana. Because I see a red-and-yellow streetcar, just like the ones they have here. And that day on the bus, when I got my first look at the city—it just felt like I'd seen it before."

They were all looking at him intently.

"Could your visions be predictions of the future?" Kick asked. "That's how it is with me. I see something and then it happens."

"I'm not sure," Cyrus answered slowly, thinking about it. "But it feels like something that's *already* happened. Something I remember."

Beatrice shot Iris a look. "That's what you said— that Cyrus was reliving something from his past."

"And there's one more thing," Cyrus said. "Besides the visions, I've been having—I guess you'd call them hallucinations. Weird ones. Almost everywhere I go, I think I see a fox."

Beatrice almost choked on a bite of slug. She managed to swallow it, and then she said, "That's no hallucination, Cyrus. I've seen the fox, too."

Cyrus's head snapped up and he looked at her eagerly. "You have? Does it sing for you, too?"

"Well, no," Beatrice said. "But I saw it three different times the day we took our entrance exams. And once, it was looking into the schoolroom, seeming to watch us. Only now I wonder if maybe it wasn't just watching you." She looked at Ollie and then Teddy. "Have either of you seen it?"

They shook their heads no.

"Cyrus, what did you mean about the fox singing?" Ollie asked.

"It throws back its head," Cyrus said, "and makes this . . . this kind of warbling sound, like a song. And then it looks at me—straight into my eyes—and seems to be trying to tell me something. I was sure I had to be imagining the whole thing because foxes don't act like that. *Do* they?"

"You aren't imagining anything," Beatrice said. "The fox I saw was real. Although," she added thoughtfully, "I do think there's something magical about it because it didn't leave paw prints in the snow and it seemed to disappear into thin air."

"And since it's followed us here—or more likely, followed *you*, Cyrus," Ollie said, "maybe it has something to do with the visions. We just need to figure out how it's all related." He turned to look at Kick. "I think it's time you told us everything you know about Widdershins."

After lunch, Cyrus left for his meeting with Mrs. Harridan and the rest of them went outside.

"Come on, I know a place where we won't be overheard," Kick said, and headed into the woods.

He took them to a clearing that was encircled by a dense wall of balsam and pine. Inside the circle of trees were large, flat rocks that were perfect for sitting.

"I found this place when I was new at Widdershins," Kick said. "I used to come here when I was homesick and wanted to be by myself."

After everyone had found a rock and sat down, Beatrice said, "Kick, before you start, we should tell you that Cadwallader filled us in on his magical intuition theory. And, in my opinion, he's just using us to prove himself."

Kick nodded. "Yep, that about sums it up."

"Plus he told us we might be working on a special assignment," Beatrice continued, "and—well, I overheard you and Axel talking about something called the Bane Project."

"Oh, but Teddy doesn't know about Bane," Ollie cut in.

"That's what witches in Arcana call the monster," Beatrice told her.

Teddy's eyes got big and she started to say something, but Beatrice had already turned back to Kick. "Anyway," she said, "we figured the Bane Project and Dr. Cadwallader's assignment must be one and the same."

"They are," Kick said. "Cadwallader's been trying to get a team together for a long time, and at the end of last semester he hinted that he might put me on it." Kick frowned. "Like I should feel honored."

"So what would the team have to do?" Beatrice asked.

"Using our magical intuition," Kick said with an ironic grimace, "we'd go down under the city and destroy the monster. And if our intuition is good enough, some of us might even get out alive."

"You mean the Department of Witch Education would approve a project like this?" Ollie asked.

"No way," Kick said. "That's why Cadwallader likes Widdershins being cut off from the rest of the Sphere— so he can test his theory to his heart's content without anyone knowing. Even inside the academy, it's a big secret. Cadwallader doesn't tell anyone except the students he selects to be on the team, and they have to swear not to talk about it. I don't think the teachers even know anything."

"But you do," Teddy pointed out.

Kick nodded. "That's because a friend of mine, Milo Weir, was assigned to it, and he told me everything. The plan was for them to sprinkle a sleeping potion on some raw meat and take it into the tunnels for the monster— you know, to knock it out—and then stab it in the heart with a sword Cadwallader was going to give them."

"But those tunnels go on for miles," Beatrice said. "How was Milo's team supposed to find the monster?"

"Cadwallader had diagrams of the tunnels, and he'd marked the route they were supposed to take."

"That first day on the bus," Beatrice said, "you dropped some diagrams."

"Yeah. Those were the ones Cadwallader gave to Milo."

"Who else was on the team?" Teddy asked.

"Axel Rathbone was being considered," Kick said, "but he was dumped because he kept goofing up. So the only team members were Milo and Sadie Arrowsmith."

"The girl who had my room last year," Beatrice said.

"And the girl who disappeared, along with Milo," Kick said softly. Then his jaw tightened and there was a flash of anger in his eyes. "The only thing Milo didn't

119

know was *when* they were supposed to go into the tunnels—because Cadwallader said they needed more people and he was still trying to put a team together. And then, one morning, Milo and Sadie just weren't here anymore."

"So you think Cadwallader sent them after Bane?" Teddy asked.

"I can't prove it," Kick admitted. "But there used to be *two* swords hanging on the wall in Cadwallader's office, and the morning we found Milo and Sadie gone, there was only one. Most people didn't question Cadwallader's story—that Milo and Sadie had left a note and run away together—but I know it didn't happen that way. What I think is, Cadwallader sent them into those tunnels alone and the monster killed them."

"But they might have run away," Teddy said. "You know, young witches in love and all that."

Kick just shook his head sadly. "Not likely. Sadie had a crush on a guy who graduated last year. And Milo—well, he was sort of a geek—and the only reason Sadie spent time with him was because of the project. Besides, Milo had it bad for another girl." He looked at Beatrice. "It was your buddy—Diantha Winter-Rose."

"And I'm guessing," Beatrice said, "that the feeling wasn't mutual. Diantha doesn't strike me as someone who'd be interested in a geek."

"She just used him," Kick said bitterly. "He gave her gifts and did her homework. And she liked him following him around like a puppy. I tried to get him to see what she was doing, but he wouldn't listen. He was head over heels in love with Diantha and wouldn't believe anything bad about her. So why would he run off with Sadie? Even if she agreed, and she wouldn't have."

"I assume the authorities looked for Sadie and Milo," Ollie said.

"Oh, yeah," Kick said, "and I guess they're still looking. They all bought into everything Cadwallader told them."

He stood up and walked over to the edge of the clearing. Standing with his back to them, he said, "I know I should have told someone, but who would believe me?" He turned around and Beatrice saw the frustration in his face. "I don't have any proof," he said, "just a missing sword and a gut feeling. That's why I was in your room, Beatrice, looking for *something*—a letter, a diary—anything she might have left that would prove she and Milo were going into those tunnels. But I didn't find anything, so it's my word against Cadwallader's. And he has powerful friends—the mayor, for one. And Januarius Moonstone, for another."

"Who's Januarius Moonstone?" Teddy asked.

"One of the richest men in the Sphere," Kick said, and pointed through the woods. "His estate's right over there." He came back and sat down, looking desolate. "I don't know what to do, but I can't just drop it. Milo deserves better than that, you know?"

"Where did you find those diagrams?" Beatrice asked.

"In Milo's room, after he disappeared."

"But wouldn't he and Sadie have needed them if they were going into the tunnels?"

"It's a straight shot," Kick said. "Once they'd seen how to go, they wouldn't have had to look at the diagrams again."

Ollie had been listening quietly. Now he said, "I know Axel wasn't involved in the project for long, but he still might know something. Or Milo might have talked to someone else. We could try to find out."

"But we don't know who we can trust," Beatrice said, "and if word got back to Cadwallader that we were snooping around about the Bane Project, we'd be in big trouble. He might even suspect that it was Kick who told us about it."

"I think you're right," Teddy said. "Cadwallader cares so much about this project, who knows what he'd do to protect the secrecy around it?"

Now Beatrice turned back to Kick. "With everything you suspect, you must detest this place. I'm not sure I would have come back."

"I didn't want to," Kick said. "But I thought, if Cadwallader assigned me to the Bane Project, maybe he'd let something slip and I'd find out what happened to Milo and Sadie."

Beatrice studied his face for a moment and then she said, "Okay, you can count me in. If Cadwallader assigns me to the project, I'll do it."

The others agreed to help, too, even Iris. But she was blinking very fast.

"And now, what about Cyrus?" Beatrice asked. "We have to do something to help him. If nothing else, get him out of here."

"Well . . .," Teddy said, "we could ask him to tell us every detail of what he sees when he's in a trance. Maybe that would give us a clue—some idea of what's causing the visions."

"Then let's go see if he's out of his meeting with Mrs. Harridan," Ollie said, absently breaking a twig off a nearby bush. "We can bring him back here to talk."

But before anyone could respond, a tree trunk suddenly leaped through the wall of evergreens into the clearing, growling like a werewolf and waving its branches in fury.

13

The Fox Spirit

T eddy screamed, but the others were struck dumb. They all stumbled back, staring wild-eyed at what appeared to be a substantial, if rather short, tree trunk jumping around them and making angry, guttural sounds. But on closer inspection, Beatrice realized that it wasn't a tree terrorizing them at all; it was an old man. He was wearing faded, grayish-brown robes and had a weathered face that bore a striking resemblance to knotty wood. And it was Ollie who seemed to be bearing the brunt of his indignation.

The tree-man had gone from jumping to stomping his feet and yelling at Ollie. By listening carefully, Beatrice caught words behind the growls and screeches.

"That bush is a living thing," the old man shouted, shaking a long, rootlike finger in Ollie's face. "And when you snapped that twig, the bush felt pain. What if I ripped your arm off? Think it would hurt? Well, that's how it feels to trees and bushes when your kind does injury to them!"

Ollie's face had turned red and he was uttering profuse apologies, which finally seemed to calm the old man down. With one last growl, he stopped pointing and stomping and just glared at Ollie.

Feeling the need to come to Ollie's defense, Beatrice said, "My friend would never hurt anything or anyone, not deliberately. But we didn't know a bush could feel pain."

"Well, now that you do," the tree-man grumbled, "remember it."

Teddy had been eyeing him with some astonishment. "If you don't mind my asking," she said, "just who are you?"

The man fixed his knotty gaze on Teddy and said with quiet dignity, "My name is Cormac and I'm one of the men-in-the-oak."

"What are the men-in-the-oak?" Beatrice asked.

"We're men who live in oak trees," Cormac answered, giving her a look that said she should have been able to figure that one out for herself. "It's our job to protect the trees and other plants—as well as the wild animals that live in the forest."

Ollie gave Kick a questioning look.

Kick said with a shrug, "This is all new to me."

Cayenne had sidled over to Cormac and was now sniffing at his skinny, brown feet. Surprisingly, the old face softened and Cormac reached down to stroke the cat's head with his gnarly fingers. Cayenne started to purr and rub against his ankles, which was the only character reference Beatrice needed.

"I'm the groundskeeper at Widdershins," Cormac added, now giving Cayenne a belly rub. "Since I was already living on the grounds—in that big, old oak over there—the headmaster decided to hire me."

"It's a lot to take care of," Ollie said.

Cormac cut his eyes at Ollie, apparently still having doubts about someone who would harm a bush, and said gruffly, "I have help."

He straightened up and leaned close to a small birch. "Tree spirits," he whispered, "be polite and show yourselves."

Two tiny heads suddenly popped out from behind a limb.

"This is Gillie," Cormac said, "and this is Perrie."

One of the creatures shinnied up the tree as fast as a squirrel and stepped into Cormac's outstretched palm. The other one settled into the fork of a branch and studied Beatrice and her friends with interest. Dressed in moss and leaves, with faces about the size and color of acorns, they seemed friendly, but shy.

"There are hundreds of tree spirits in these woods," Cormac said, "and I couldn't do my job without them."

Beatrice was fascinated by the man-in-the-oak, and charmed by Gillie and Perrie, but something else was on her mind. "Mr. Cormac—"

"It's just Cormac," the old man said gruffly.

"All right, Cormac, and I'm Beatrice. I was just wondering if you've noticed a fox around here."

"Foxes come along from time to time," he said, "but lately, there's just been the one fox spirit."

"Fox *spirit?* What's that?"

"Any fox can become a fox spirit," he told her, "if it lives long enough. And then it can live hundreds of years."

"Even a thousand," said the creature in his hand.

"That's right, Perrie," Cormac said in his gravelly voice, looking amused as the tree spirit scampered up his arm to sit on his shoulder. "All fox spirits are female—though I couldn't say why—and the only way you can tell them from an ordinary fox is if you see them doing their magic, like beating their tails on the ground to start a fire. But what's most unique is how the spirits of the dead can pass into a fox spirit—and often do."

"Why would they want to?" Teddy asked.

"Because they have unfinished business here on Earth," Cormac said, "and the fox spirit can help them take care of it. But just as every witch and every man-in-the-oak has a different personality, so does the fox spirit. Some are tricksters, just wanting a good laugh, while others go out of their way to make trouble for people. Then we have fox spirits who right the wrongs of the world. I call these avengers. And the one hanging around here? She's an avenger, all right, but a gentle one. Here for a purpose, that's for sure, the way she keeps coming back day after day, just standing there for hours looking up at the school."

This has to be Cyrus's fox, Beatrice thought—*or, rather, fox spirit.*

"That's odd behavior for her kind," Cormac continued, "since they don't usually linger in one place for long. Fox spirits are wanderers at heart, you see, and only stay as long as they need to."

After breakfast the next morning, Beatrice and the other students were streaming down the wide staircase to the basement for their first class. Beatrice's mouth was dry and her stomach was doing flip-flops. She was no good at magic—*that* was a proven fact—so what if she ended up making a complete fool of herself? She could see it all now: Her classmates snickering, her teachers losing their patience—and *then*, Dr. Cadwallader sending her home in disgrace.

She glanced at Ollie beside her and saw that he looked nervous, too. Then he winked at her and said, "Think positive. Everything's going to be fine."

"I'm sure it will be," Beatrice said, trying hard to believe it.

But just then another student bumped into her and Beatrice grabbed for the stair rail to keep from stumbling. And as her fingers closed around the railing, the cold, hard stone seemed to disintegrate beneath them, becoming soft and mushy—and wiggly!

Beatrice glanced down and then jerked her hand away in horror. The spot she'd touched had been transformed into a pink, pulpy mass of worms!

Other students saw the squirming blob and started to shriek and babble. Cyrus drew back and Teddy exclaimed, "How *revolting!*"

Then Beatrice noticed a glistening, flesh-colored worm clinging to her palm. She flung out her hand to shake it loose and struck the armload of books Iris had clasped to her chest. And the instant Beatrice's hand made contact with the books, they dissolved into a greenish-yellow slime that poured down the front of Iris's sweater.

Iris gave a bloodcurdling scream and everyone jumped away from her, staring in disgust at the pool of mucus collecting on the stairs at her feet. Starting to cry, she pulled a wad of tissues from her pocket and started dabbing at the gunk on her clothes, her eyes blinking nonstop. And Beatrice just stared at her, speechless, trying desperately to understand what was happening. She had a sense that she was somehow responsible, but—what exactly had she done to cause this mess?

Weak-kneed and feeling a little sick, Beatrice leaned against the stair rail, and—wouldn't you know it?—as soon as her hand touched it, she felt something wet on her fingers. When she looked, she saw blood running in a stream along the railing and dripping in big, crimson splotches onto the steps.

"Beatrice!" Teddy screeched. "What's going *on?* Everything you touch turns into—something horrible!"

Just then Dr. Cadwallader pushed his way down the stairs through the crush of students until he reached Beatrice. That's when a female voice shouted out, *"She* did it! Her idea of a joke, I guess." Beatrice jerked her head toward the voice and saw Diantha Winter-Rose pointing an accusing finger at her.

Looking back at Dr. Cadwallader, who was glaring into her face, Beatrice sputtered, "I—I didn't do it on purpose. Honest! I don't know *what* made it happen."

The headmaster's dark eyes shifted with distaste to the puddles of clotting blood and greenish slime, and to the fist-sized ball of wriggling worms that had landed near his left foot. Then he muttered something under his breath and, suddenly, it was all gone. The handrail and steps were clean, the slime was gone from Iris's clothes, and there wasn't so much as a speck of blood on Beatrice's hand.

"I really didn't do anything," Beatrice said miserably.

"I believe you, Miss Bailiwick," the headmaster said, although his voice was curt and far from reassuring. "It appears that you were hexed."

Beatrice heard a collective intake of breath around her and then whispered chatter.

"But why would anyone hex Beatrice?" Teddy asked.

"There could be a dozen reasons," Dr. Cadwallader barked with an angry shake of his head. "Of greater concern to me is why the spells I have in place to protect the academy don't seem to be working. No one should be able to place a hex on anyone within these walls. They'd have to know the protective spells I used in order to override them."

Now the headmaster was looking suspiciously at the faces around him, as if searching out an enemy among them. Then he scowled and said in a booming voice, "All right, we've wasted enough time for one morning. Everyone get to class. Now!"

Beatrice's nerves were shot when she walked into her Intuitive Magic class. Who could be doing this? The same person who put maggots in her cereal, most likely!

They were the kind of petty, immature pranks that another kid might pull—a *vicious* one, in need of immediate help! Someone like Diantha Winter-Rose, maybe? Or was it more serious than that? Were these tricks just nasty warnings of worse to come?

As she sat down, surrounded by her friends, Beatrice apologized to Iris for the third time and Iris said kindly, "I know it wasn't you, Beatrice. So forget it, okay?"

Beatrice didn't think it likely that she'd ever forget the sight of poor Iris covered in slime, and wondering what might come *next* had her rattled. But she tried to pretend that this was just like any other first day of school—which was kind of hard to do when she looked around the classroom. It was a cold, dark pit, with rickety desks covered in cobwebs and one bare bulb hanging from the ceiling that did nothing to dispel the gloom. And then there was their teacher.

Magical Intuition was taught by Dr. Petronilla Puffin, who was standing up front shuffling through her notes. She was a big woman, her sturdy frame draped in layers of ancient cloth—dark red robes over black ones, with a bit of deep purple thrown in—and she had a tangle of faded chestnut hair piled on top of her head that was managing to escape its knot one frizzy and determined tendril at a time. In short, Petronilla Puffin could do with a makeover.

But Beatrice had observed the teachers during meals, and she'd noticed that Dr. Puffin always appeared unruffled and self-assured. When she'd walk into the dining room with that wiry hair sticking out in all directions, eyes would follow her. She had what Teddy called presence. And despite the fact that the witch never smiled—and wasn't the least bit attractive—there was something solid and trustworthy about her that made Beatrice think of Dr. Featherstone.

Students were whispering to one another and rustling parchment as they prepared to take notes, but then Dr. Puffin's head came up and the room was instantly silent. She had a no-nonsense air about her that made even the most incorrigible chatterboxes clamp their mouths shut.

She called the roll—which didn't take long, since there were only a dozen students in the class—and then launched into a long definition of magical intuition. All summed up, Dr. Cadwallader's theory was nothing more than knowing something when there was no way you could have known it. Then Dr. Puffin gave them some history on the subject, never mentioning the headmaster by name, just using phrases like, *experts believe . . . or, those who have made the study of magical intuition their life's work presume . . .*

And then, about two minutes before the end-of-class trumpet sounded, Dr. Puffin made an announcement.

"Since you won't be starting your fieldwork yet, I've planned some outings for that time. This afternoon we'll be visiting a place that I'm sure you'll all find fascinating. So meet me in front of the building after lunch."

Their next class was Clairvoyance, which couldn't have been more different. The teacher was Dr. Deja Hawthorn, who was plump and pretty and smiled entirely too much. She informed the class that this was her first teaching job and then giggled. The class was larger, with several older students joining them, including—to Teddy's dismay—Diantha Winter-Rose. The girl scowled faintly at Beatrice and Teddy, then gave Ollie a radiant smile. Luckily, all the desks around them were taken, so Diantha had to sit on the other side of the room. A few minutes later, when Beatrice cut her eyes that way, she saw that Diantha had fallen asleep. And their giggly teacher didn't seem to have noticed.

But Dr. Hawthorn's class turned out to be fun. Instead of making them take tons of notes, she demonstrated different ways of seeing into the future. Muttering a charm under her breath, she came over to Teddy with a handful of smooth stones and threw them like dice onto Teddy's desk.

"These are the ancient rune stones," Dr. Hawthorn informed them. "I don't know this girl, but I'll be able to tell her future simply by reading how the runes have fallen."

The teacher's reading was brief and to the point. Teddy would have a spectacular future, with wealth, accomplishment, and much acclaim. She would marry well and have five children who would make her proud.

Beatrice didn't need to throw the runes to predict Diantha's reaction to this: She was furious. But Teddy was beaming, confident that the life she'd always dreamed of had just been handed to her by this woman, whom she later declared—repeatedly—to be brilliant!

Their next class was Countermagic and Protection with Dr. Upson Downs. He was the young teacher with red hair that Beatrice had noticed laughing and talking at the faculty table. And that was exactly what he did through most of the class. But by the end of the hour, they had all created Pentacles of Protection to defend themselves against magical attack, as well as a multi-purpose herbal mixture that Dr. Downs said was indispensable.

"Sprinkle some on your doorstep and your home is protected from curses," he informed them, grinning. "Sprinkle it in your bath and you're relieved of the pain and itching of sunburn, bee stings, and hemorrhoids."

Their last class before lunch was Seasons of Magic, taught by Dr. Hugo Shambelly. The teacher was a mountain of a man, with very little hair on his head and an abundance of it trailing out of his nostrils. First he called the roll, then talked a few minutes about his stock portfolio, and then told them to read Chapter One in their textbooks. "Pay close attention to the festival of Midsummer Eve," he advised them with a sly wink. "A little pixie told me that might show up on a pop quiz tomorrow."

Everyone groaned and reached for their books, while Dr. Shambelly opened *Witch Business Weekly*, which he read until the trumpet sounded.

On their way to the dining room for lunch, Beatrice glanced at Teddy, who hadn't stopped grinning since Dr. Hawthorn had announced her glorious future. "So what did you think of the morning, Teddy?"

"Brilliant," Teddy answered happily. "That woman is absolutely brilliant."

14

Moonstone

While Beatrice and her friends were eating a hearty lunch of roasted frog's bladder in woolly warm sauce, Mrs. Harridan stopped by their table and said to Cyrus in her usual frosty manner, "It's best that you don't go on the field trip with Dr. Puffin's class this afternoon. We wouldn't want you having any problems away from school, now would we?"

Once she was gone, Beatrice said, "That is so unfair! Cyrus, you haven't had a vision since the first night. *Have* you?" she added tentatively.

Cyrus shook his head. "No, but I don't care. You're probably just going to a museum or something."

So after lunch, Cyrus and Kick headed for the gym to shoot baskets and the rest of the Magical Intuition class gathered outside on the front steps. Beatrice had expected to see the *Happy Hills* bus pull up, but when Dr. Puffin came through the door, she said briskly, "Follow me, class," and took off on foot around the side of the building. Beatrice noticed that she was wearing what looked like combat boots under her ragtag robes, which turned out to be a practical choice since the

135

teacher proceeded to lead them across the back lawn and into the woods.

Beatrice and her friends were at the end of a single-file line following a narrow path that wound through the trees. As they moved deeper into the woods, Beatrice kept her eyes open for Cormac and the tree spirits, but the forest was hushed and still. Before long, the path became overgrown with underbrush and trees closed in around them so they had to push through branches in order to pass. It was at this point that a disgruntled Cayenne leaped up out of the briars and brambles to Beatrice's shoulder.

"Ouch!" one of the students yelled as a thorny bush raked his face.

"Not much farther now," Dr. Puffin said over her shoulder.

"What could we possibly be seeing in the middle of the woods?" Iris wondered aloud.

Then the trees began to thin out and the path became visible again. And Beatrice realized that the forest was no longer silent. Up ahead, she could hear what sounded like animal noises: snarls and yelps and growls.

Teddy whispered to Beatrice, "Do you think Dr. Puffin's aware of all the critters in these woods?"

Beatrice looked back over her shoulder to respond, and that's when something so amazing caught her eye, she came to a dead stop. Just behind Teddy and Ollie was a good-sized maple tree, and stretched out on one of its lower limbs, about three feet above their heads, was the most incredible-looking lizard Beatrice had ever seen. It had to be at least five feet long and its scaly body

136

was the bright yellow of summer squash, with darker shades of orange and gold along its ridged back. Beatrice was close enough to see the creature's tack-sharp claws clinging to the tree bark and the glittering intensity in its small, hooded eyes—eyes that seemed to be staring directly into her face.

"Don't make any sudden moves," she whispered. "Just turn around slowly and look."

"Look at what?" Teddy asked, as both she and Ollie swiveled their heads toward the maple tree—and froze.

Teddy let out a startled squawk, just as Ollie said in a low, strained voice, "Do you know what that is? I've seen pictures. It's a frothy-mouth dragon. And they breathe out foam instead of fire—but it's poisonous. If one drop hits you, you're dead."

Perched on Beatrice's shoulder, Cayenne was staring at the dragon, too, and growling deep in her throat.

"Back away," Ollie said softly. "Frothy-mouths are leapers, not runners. Once we're out of its line of vision, we should be safe."

The creature was still watching Beatrice with its gleaming, pinpoint eyes as they took a step back. And it was at that critical, and ill-timed, moment that Dr. Puffin called out, "Miss Bailiwick! What are you people doing back there? Come along now, stay with the group."

Before they could answer, the frothy-mouth leaped—sailing at lightning speed over Teddy and Ollie's heads, straight at Beatrice!

It hit her chest with such force, she was knocked to the ground and then pinned down by its enormous weight. She could feel those claws, like a dozen tiny knives, cutting through her jacket into her shoulders. She could see the yellow blur of its reptilian face only inches from her own, its jaw working in a furious chewing motion. And in a moment of mindless terror, she screamed, only it came out as a breathless whimper.

Hearing the angry hissing of a cat near her ear, Beatrice cried out, "Cayenne! Stay away!"

Her vision was blocked by the dragon, but now she could hear the sounds of movement around her. Frantic whispering, then feet shuffling and the crackling of dead leaves. And all of a sudden the weight on her body shifted, first to one side and then the other, as if someone was trying to roll the frothy-mouth off her. And out of the corner of her eye, she saw what looked like a limb being raised in the air, then lowered—fast and hard— onto the dragon's head.

Beatrice felt the impact of that blow all through her body, stunning her. But then the weight on her chest suddenly lifted, allowing her, at last, to take a deep breath. And that's when she saw the dragon, not three feet away, rearing up on its hind legs as if to attack—and Ollie approaching the beast, muttering, his hands heaped with dirty snow.

The next thing Beatrice knew, Ollie was flinging melted snow into the dragon's face. Then the creature screamed in agony, a nasty brown foam bubbling out of it's mouth before it dropped to all four feet and took off, still howling, into the trees.

Silence followed, with Beatrice looking up into the ring of faces staring down at her. Teddy. Ollie. Cyrus.

Cayenne. Iris. Dr. Puffin. And the rest of the class, whose names she hadn't learned yet.

"Beatrice, are you okay?" Teddy asked anxiously. She was holding a thick limb like a baseball bat and breathing hard.

"You knocked it off me," Beatrice said, struggling to sit up.

"Hit it between the eyes," Teddy said with a sudden grin. "Then Ollie scooped up snow and did his boiling spell. *That's* what saved you," she added with uncharacteristic humility.

Cayenne crawled into Beatrice's lap and Beatrice hugged her.

"Are you sure you're all right?" Dr. Puffin asked. Then she shook her head, seeming puzzled. "Who would have thought we'd ever see a frothy-mouth dragon in these parts? They're indigenous to the mountains in the west, where it's hot. This climate doesn't agree with them at all."

"Would it have killed her?" one of the boys asked with a curious glance at Beatrice.

"Oh, yes." Dr. Puffin nodded solemnly. "These dragons agitate their jaws to turn their saliva into a thick froth, and then they spit it on their victims. It's quite deadly." She was looking intently at Beatrice again. "I just wonder why it went after you specifically, Miss Bailiwick."

"But wouldn't it have attacked anyone who crossed its path?" Beatrice asked her.

"Frothy-mouths can leap great distances," Dr. Puffin said, "but they're one of the laziest creatures in the

Sphere. So invariably, they'll go after the closest prey. But this one chose to leap *over* two perfectly good dinners," she added, glancing at Teddy and Ollie, "to reach *you*, Miss Bailiwick."

"You said *chose*, as if they can make intelligent decisions," Ollie said. "But I remember reading that they're not very bright."

"You're correct, Mr. Tibbs." The teacher gave him an approving nod. "They're incredibly stupid. But every living thing can be—*manipulated*."

Beatrice gave her a sharp look. "You mean, bewitched? You think someone sent that dragon after me?"

Dr. Puffin frowned. "I don't know what to think, my dear. You *were* the target of a hex this morning."

Seeing the worry in Beatrice's face, Dr. Puffin patted her arm and said quickly, "But I could be all wrong about that. There could be a very different explanation for the frothy-mouth showing up here and attacking you instead of Miss Berry or Mr. Tibbs. So—do you feel like continuing on? If you'd rather go back to the academy, someone can walk with you."

"No, I'm fine," Beatrice said as she stood up. "I want to go on."

"All right then," Dr. Puffin said briskly. "Line up, class, we're almost there. Just stay together this time. And watch out for anything lurking—especially if it's bright yellow."

Beatrice couldn't be sure, but she thought the teacher meant that as a joke.

As they started down the path again, Beatrice said to Teddy and Ollie, "Thanks, you guys. You saved me."

"But what was that frothy thing doing here?" Teddy mused. "Beatrice, I'm beginning to think someone *has* targeted you—and it's getting out of hand. A bowl of maggots is one thing, but that dragon could have *killed* you."

"Well, it didn't," Beatrice said, and then added in a tight voice, "I'm not worried."

A few minutes later, she realized what their destination would be when she caught sight of a giant stone arch through the trees, with a sign above it that read: *Moonstone Wildlife Preserve.* Through the arch she could see rolling hills—brilliantly green, in the middle of winter!—and off to one side, craggy purple cliffs rising into the clouds. And all of it was bathed in a golden light that seemed brighter than ordinary sunshine.

Dr. Puffin stopped in front of the arch and turned to the class. Her face was flushed and her hair looked more alarming than ever as she said, "Mr. Januarius Moonstone opened this wildlife preserve more than a decade ago for the purpose of saving rare and endangered animals. And each semester he allows the teachers at Widdershins to bring new students here for a tour of the facility. It's a once-in-a-lifetime opportunity. Today you'll observe, firsthand, animals that most witches can only read about."

The students began to talk excitedly among themselves and Dr. Puffin said sharply, "Quiet, please! One of Mr. Moonstone's employees will be here shortly to take us through the preserve. While we wait for him, I'd like to give you some background. As some of you may know, Mr. Moonstone is a businessman in the Arcana community. He has a clothing line called, appropriately enough, Moonstone. His robes and cloaks and other traditional witchwear are sold in better stores throughout the Sphere."

"I just *adore* them," one of the girls gushed. "All my new birthday clothes are Moonstone."

Dr. Puffin gave the girl a testy look before continuing. "Mr. Januarius Moonstone is a good friend of Widdershins Academy, and a good neighbor, as well. His home is nearby, bordering Arcana and Widdershins, and is recognized by the Witches' Sphere Historical Society as a national landmark. But the true and enduring passion of Mr. Moonstone's life is saving animals from neglect and abuse. I can't think of anyone who has done more for these vulnerable and exquisite creatures."

"My dear Dr. Puffin," came a voice from behind her, "you flatter me."

A man in rich gold robes that were lined with scarlet silk came striding through the arches toward them. He had black, wavy hair with gray at the temples, a lean smiling face, and alert dark eyes that took them all in with one sweeping glance.

"Why—Mr. Moonstone," Dr. Puffin said in surprise, "I didn't expect to see you here today. Class, isn't this a treat?"

"How wonderful to have you all here," Mr. Moonstone said, beaming. "I can't tell you how happy it makes me to see young people showing an interest in animals."

"It's so good of you to take the time to meet our new students," Dr. Puffin said. "I know how busy you are. With factories all over the Sphere, you're away quite a bit, aren't you?"

"Yes, unfortunately, my business does keep me on the road more than I'd like," he answered, "although I'm grateful that I live outside the city limits so that I *can* travel and keep an eye on things. It's the clothing line that's allowed me to build and operate this sanctuary for the animals." He turned back to the students and said, "But since I'm here today, why don't I take you on the tour myself?"

Just then, a long, open vehicle that resembled a golf cart, but with a string of extra seats, pulled up to the arch. A young man in khaki robes got out, and that's when Beatrice noticed that the cart didn't have wheels. But then, it didn't need them; instead of moving *across* the ground, the vehicle floated a few inches above it.

"Gabe, I'll do the honors today," Mr. Moonstone said to his employee. "All right, kids, hop into the cart and we'll be on our way."

They all clambered aboard, with Dr. Puffin sitting next to Mr. Moonstone up front, and Beatrice and Ollie just behind them. Teddy and Iris found seats further back.

"Everyone ready?" Mr. Moonstone called out. Then he raised his hand and the cart moved silently forward, floating through the archway and into the wildlife preserve.

Beatrice realized at once that the light *was* different here, casting a golden glow as rich as wild honey across the hills. And the hills, themselves, were as soft as plump cushions and vividly green—the dazzling green of spring—no, of a *thousand* springs.

"This place has been enchanted," Ollie whispered to her. "The light, the sky . . ."

Beatrice lifted her face to look and the blue overhead was so brilliant, it hurt her eyes. "It's—breathtaking," she said softly.

"It is," Ollie agreed. "He's created a paradise for these animals."

They were following a path that wound across the hills in the direction of the cliffs, a path paved with white, iridescent stones that caught the light like fiery opals. Beatrice was completely absorbed in her surroundings, as was Cayenne, but for a different reason. The cat had slid off Beatrice's lap and was hanging out of the cart, sniffing the air as she picked up one irresistible animal scent after another.

Ahead was a large, blue-green pond nestled between two emerald hills. Beatrice had just noticed the animals at the edge of the water when Mr. Moonstone's voice sounded over a speaker.

"Here you see several species living peacefully together," he said. "Look first at the black stallion over there."

Standing alone, his long neck lowered gracefully to drink, was the largest, most beautiful horse Beatrice had ever seen. And, incredibly, the animal had eight legs!

"This horse is very rare," Mr. Moonstone told them. "He's descended from Sleipir, the Norse god Odin's horse—who also has eight legs. The people I send out to rescue animals go to the ends of the earth to find them, even to the mortal world. That's where they discovered this magnificent creature. And now, if you'll turn your attention to the dogs."

Lying side by side on a ledge of rock that jutted into the water were two enormous canines, one black and one white. They had massive heads and paws the size of catchers' mitts.

"These dogs," Mr. Moonstone said, "are the off-spring of Spitak, the white dog of life, and Siaw, the black dog of death. According to mortal myth, the black dog carries off mortals to die and the white dog can, if it so chooses, restore them back to life." Mr. Moonstone sighed. "But as we all know, mortals don't appreciate—often, don't even *believe in*—the magical beasts from their myths, and many are disgracefully neglected when we find them. These pups, for example, were on the brink of death when we brought them here, but our devoted staff has worked tirelessly to save them."

Then Mr. Moonstone pointed out wild cats swimming in the water and sunning on the rocks. "An ancestor of the big tiger that just dove in," he said, "pulled the Roman god Juno's chariot."

For the next hour, the cart meandered across the green hills and along the base of the cliffs—rugged, plum-colored spires of rock that shot skyward until they pierced the clouds. Beatrice and her classmates saw hundreds of animals—dogs, cats, wolves, birds—all descended from magical creatures that were famous and rare.

Even though Beatrice couldn't help thinking that none of the creatures seemed quite as exotic—not to mention, terrifying—as a certain yellow dragon, the tour of the preserve was an extraordinary experience. And when the cart finally pulled through the archway and came to a stop, no one spoke. But as they stepped out onto the winter-brown grass, into sunlight that suddenly seemed dull and ordinary, the spell of the enchanted place began to fade and the students found their voices. Over their excited chatter, Dr. Puffin was thanking Mr. Moonstone, and that's when Beatrice saw it. Not ten feet away, hidden among the gnarled roots of an ancient oak tree, was the fox.

"Ollie, look," she said.

Mr. Moonstone, who was standing nearby, turned in the direction she was pointing.

"Oh, that," he said, without much interest. "It's just a fox spirit. They're fairly common, even in the mortal world." Then he added to Dr. Puffin, "I wouldn't have gone out seeking one, but she just showed up a few days ago and we let her stay. I'm surprised she's still here. As you probably know, fox spirits rarely linger in one place for long."

15

The Lion That Flew

When Beatrice and her friends got back from the wildlife preserve, they ran into Zipporah Spitz in the front hall on her way to the kitchen.

The woman's face broke into a big smile and she said, "I haven't seen you around lately." Her smile dimmed when she added, "But I heard about your friend's problems. I'm sorry he's having such a rough time."

Beatrice said, "He seems to be doing better now."

"Well, I have just the thing to help him along," Zipporah said. "Mayfly pie. Nobody can stay down for long when they're eating my pie."

So Ollie went to get Cyrus, and ten minutes later they were all sitting at the long oak table eating pie while Zipporah cooked dinner and Cayenne lapped up a bowl of curdled cream custard.

"This is good," Cyrus said, sounding surprised.

Zipporah beamed at him. "Mayfly is my speciality," she said. Then she gave him a long, thoughtful look. "You're a skinny little thing, aren't you? I need to start fattening you up."

"It must be a lot of work cooking for so many people," Ollie said. "You don't have any help?"

"Just the Ellyons," Zipporah answered as she stirred a pot on the stove. She looked up and saw their blank faces. "Elves," she added. "They wash dishes and clean up for me, but they'll only come in after everyone's gone to bed. Shy, you know. And if they think somebody's spying on them, they disappear for good." Zipporah frowned. "It seems like I'm always running help-wanted ads in *The Elf Examiner*."

Still attacking his pie with gusto, Cyrus said, "Ollie told me you guys went to some animal place today."

"Yeah," Teddy said. "It was really cool."

Zipporah had lifted her head again to look at them. "This wouldn't be the Moonstone Wildlife Preserve, would it?"

"That's right," Beatrice answered, wondering at the sudden alertness in Zipporah's face. "Have you been there?"

"No," Zipporah said quickly, "I haven't."

She took several loaves of bread out of the oven and brought them over to the table. Watching her, Beatrice thought she seemed preoccupied, like her mind was miles away.

Zipporah started slicing the bread. "I used to work for Mr. Moonstone and his wife," she said. "But that was a long time ago."

Beatrice was still watching Zipporah, thinking, *She's upset about something.*

"Zipporah, are you okay?" Beatrice asked.

"What? Oh, sure," Zipporah said. "It's just . . . thinking about the Moonstones makes me sad, is all." And she might have left it at that if she hadn't noticed the five pairs of curious eyes on her.

"I was very fond of Mrs. Moonstone," she explained, and then that faraway look came back to her face. "Liliana was her name. She was so lovely, with the most beautiful blue eyes. And that laugh of hers! Just being around her made you feel good."

Beatrice had noticed that Zipporah was talking about Liliana Moonstone in the past tense, so she wasn't surprised when the woman said heavily, "It was a terrible thing, her dying. I'll never forget that night."

Then Zipporah shook her head, as if trying to clear it of these unwelcome thoughts, and went back to slicing the bread. "Liliana was a descendent of the great fairy king Finvarra," she said. "Some witches look down on fairies, but they have a very old and rich history."

"Liliana must not have been the same kind of fairy as Rhude and Rankin," Iris guessed.

This brought a faint smile to Zipporah's lips. "No," she said. "The branch descended from Finvarra is at the top of the fairy scale. Liliana was proud of her heritage—she even named her son Finvarra for his famous ancestor—and her family never understood why she'd marry a witch when she could have had her pick of suitors from the fairy world. But Liliana didn't have a prejudiced bone in her body. Witch, fairy, elf—she didn't see any difference. That tells you what kind of person she was."

"So what happened to her?" Teddy asked.

"She was killed by the monster," Zipporah said in a flat voice. "That first night, after Rollo Grubbs had sent witches in to destroy it, the beast came up from the caverns. It shook the whole city, causing buildings to collapse. Liliana was found under a pile of rubble."

They were all looking at her with horrified expressions.

"And her son?" Beatrice said softly. "What happened to him?"

Zipporah sighed. "The monster took Finvarra down into the caverns, as it did so many others. And none of them has ever been seen again."

It was a quiet dinner for Beatrice and her friends. After they'd told Kick about Liliana Moonstone and her son, no one felt much like talking. Beatrice noticed absently that Januarius Moonstone and Rollo Grubbs were at the faculty table, but she didn't give it much thought until they were leaving the dining room. That's when the mayor grabbed hold of her arm and exclaimed, "Well, if it isn't Beatrice Bailiwick! I'd recognize you anywhere, with that red hair and the cat perched on your shoulder!"

Dr. Cadwallader was standing just behind the mayor, all puffed up and looking smug, and Januarius Moonstone was smiling at Beatrice with polite, if limited, interest.

"Hodge, old man, this is quite a coup for Widdershins," Rollo Grubbs said, his eyes bugging out at Beatrice. "So tell me, my dear, have you found the academy to your liking? Are they taking good care of you?"

"Yes, sir," Beatrice murmured.

With his face only inches away from hers, she'd discovered two things about the man: He had very bad breath and his booming voice made her eardrums vibrate. Not only that, but he was gripping her arm so tightly, the huge diamond ring on his finger was cutting into her skin.

"And have you had time to tour our beautiful city?" he bellowed. "You'll find everything you need here. Stores, restaurants, dentists—"

"Monsters," Teddy said cheerfully.

The mayor's head jerked in her direction, and Dr. Cadwallader's pride turned to instant disapproval.

"Um—It was a joke," Teddy said, and chuckled unconvincingly.

"A very poor one," the headmaster snapped.

Somewhat recovered, Rollo Grubbs gave Teddy an imitation of a smile and said, "But we need to keep our sense of humor, Hodge—especially in times of adversity. Of course," he added, giving Teddy a hard, bug-eyed look, "it's easy to be flippant when you've never actually *seen* the monster."

"And you have?" Teddy asked, apparently forgetting that she was already treading on thin ice. "Seen the monster, I mean."

"Miss Berry—" Dr. Cadwallader started, but Rollo Grubbs held up his hand to shush the headmaster.

"No, no, Hodge, it's all right," the mayor said. "I don't mind satisfying this young witch's curiosity. And yes, my dear, I *did* see the monster. The first time it ever surfaced. What a horrible night that was," he muttered, shaking his head. "Walls toppling, fires blazing, people panicking—it was something you'd better hope you never experience."

"But *the monster*," Teddy prompted. "You said you saw it."

Beatrice was trying hard not to smile. Teddy's audacity never failed to amaze her.

"Yes, I did," Rollo Grubbs answered. "It was coming down the street straight for me—while I was rescuing some little children from its path."

Not likely, Beatrice thought. She'd only known the man for a few minutes, but she had the feeling that the only way he would have encountered the monster was when he was running away from it. *Rescuing little children*. It was all Beatrice could do to keep from rolling her eyes.

"So what did it look like?" Kick asked the mayor.

Rollo Grubbs frowned. "Well, it was dark, so I couldn't see much—just the size of it as it crushed vehicles under its feet. Believe me, this thing is huge!"

"And I understand you feed it now to keep it happy," Teddy said.

"To keep it *controlled*," the mayor corrected. "Workers take bags of raw meat to the tunnel entrance every morning, which doesn't come cheap, let me tell you. But the witches of Arcana would rather pay for that than have the beast come out of its lair and drag them off."

About that time, Beatrice realized that Ollie was no longer beside her. When she looked around, she saw him standing outside the dining room with Diantha. The girl was smiling and talking with a good deal of animation. But what surprised Beatrice was how Ollie was giving Diantha his full attention, as if she were the most interesting person he'd ever met.

"Come on, Rollo," Dr. Cadwallader said gruffly. "You're here to play cards, remember?"

Beatrice thought she heard Rollo Grubbs say something to her before he left, but she wasn't really listening. She was too busy watching as Ollie and Diantha started down the hall together.

When Beatrice came back downstairs with her books and laptop, her friends were already sitting in a corner of the crowded lounge. There was a seat next to Ollie on the couch, but Beatrice took a chair some distance away. He gave her a surprised look, which she chose to ignore.

"Cyrus, I thought we'd be able to talk to you about your—well, you know," Teddy said quietly, "but we need privacy for that."

"Let's get our homework out of the way," Kick said, "then take a stroll around the grounds. No one can overhear us outside."

"Stroll the grounds in the dark?" Teddy asked.

"It's safe," Kick assured her.

"Yeah, Teddy," Iris said, "don't forget those fierce sky dancers."

Everyone laughed—except for Ollie, who was focused on Beatrice and clearly puzzled, and Beatrice, herself, who was bent over her computer.

"Any quick-mails from Miranda?" Teddy asked casually.

"Eight," Beatrice answered.

Teddy's eyebrows shot up. "Then things must be going really well or really badly. Which is it?"

Beatrice blew her bangs out of her eyes and scanned down the first screen. "She loves Honoria Wagstaffe."

"That figures," Teddy muttered. "What else?"

Beatrice opened the next message. "She's already started her field assignment, working one afternoon a week at the Witches' Institute."

Teddy groaned. "Oh, *man!* And I suppose she loves that, too."

"Bingo," Beatrice said. At any other time, she might have felt sorry for Teddy, but tonight she had other things on her mind and didn't try especially hard to spare her friend's feelings. "She's even run into Dr. Featherstone."

"How very nice for her," Teddy said, and slammed a book shut.

16

Zipporah's Story

*I*n class the next morning, Dr. Puffin said briskly, "All right, today we're going to do an experiment that illustrates how magical intuition works. I'll need a volunteer."

Several hands went up.

"I believe Miss Berry was the first to raise her hand," Dr. Puffin said. "Come up front, my dear, and we'll begin."

Appearing confident that she was about to shine, a smiling Teddy came forward. Meanwhile, their teacher had brought out what looked like a deck of oversized cards.

"I have twenty-five cards here," Dr. Puffin told the class, "and each one has a drawing on it. A pentagram, a crescent moon, a cauldron, crossed broomsticks, or a witch's hat. What I'm going to do, Miss Berry, is hold up one card at a time. The class will be able to see the drawing, but you won't. And I'll ask you to tell me what the picture is on that card. The odds of you guessing correctly are one in four, or 25 percent. If you score higher than that, we can assume that something more than chance is at work—or what we call magical intuition. Now turn and face the wall, Miss Berry."

Dr. Puffin held up a card with a picture of crossed broomsticks on it. Teddy said it was a witch's hat. The teacher held up a crescent moon. Teddy guessed it was a cauldron.

After she'd gone through the entire deck, Dr. Puffin said, "Out of twenty-five cards, you named five correctly, Miss Berry. That's one in five, or 20 percent, which is actually lower than we would have expected. But don't feel bad, this is just one experiment. It doesn't necessarily mean that you have less magical intuition than someone else."

Even so, Teddy was clearly dejected as she walked back to her desk. Then the teacher tried the experiment again, this time with a boy named Rufus who got eleven out of twenty-five, or 44 percent, right. Even Dr. Puffin couldn't hide the fact that she was impressed, and Beatrice knew how hard this had to be for Teddy, who was used to being the class star.

"This experiment shows us how we can sometimes *know* things," Dr. Puffin said, "even when logic tells us that's impossible. Everyone has intuitive gifts and we can all learn how to tap into those gifts more effectively. That's what this class is all about."

Teddy was slumped down in her desk and didn't appear to be listening, but most of the students were excited by Rufus's success. They were asking when the rest of them would get a turn with the cards and if there were other ways to measure their magical intuition.

Then a boy in the back asked, "When do we start our fieldwork?"

"You have a lot to learn before you can even think about applying the theories of magical intuition in the field," Dr. Puffin said, as if she found the question faintly irritating. "From today's experiment, you may have gotten the impression that it's some sort of parlor game. Well, it isn't. It's very serious business. Because *no one* understands exactly what it is or where it comes from."

Not even Dr. Cadwallader? Beatrice wondered. It was his theory, after all. And this left her wondering how much Dr. Puffin and the other teachers knew about the headmaster's special project. Did they have any idea that he might be sending students to their deaths?

In Clairvoyance, Dr. Hawthorn started the unit on tarot card reading, with everyone scribbling to write down the lengthy, and often contradictory, meanings of the major cards. Once, when Beatrice paused to give her cramped fingers a rest, she saw Diantha snoozing again. But then Dr. Hawthorn moved on to describing ways to spread cards for a reading and Beatrice forgot about the girl. That is, until class was over, and Diantha made a beeline for Ollie.

What happened next was the last thing Beatrice would have expected. First, Ollie gave Diantha a big smile, like he was really glad to see her, and then they walked out together—just like that—without Ollie saying a word to Beatrice.

The classroom emptied quickly, leaving only Beatrice, Cyrus, Teddy, and Iris—none of whom had moved since watching Ollie and Diantha leave.

As usual, Teddy was the first to speak. She looked at Beatrice and said, "Um—I haven't wanted to say anything—"

"Then don't," Beatrice said curtly.

She gathered up her books, placed Cayenne on her shoulder, and started for the door. Ollie and Diantha were standing together in the hall and Beatrice caught a glimpse of them laughing before she turned abruptly and headed outside.

She wasn't thinking about where she was going, just that she had to get out of there. Because she was upset, and didn't want the whole world knowing it, especially Ollie.

Okay, be reasonable, Beatrice told herself as she came around the side of the building. *He's entitled to have friends besides me. He should have other friends.*

But it was obvious that Ollie was thinking of Diantha as more than just a friend. Why else would he be falling all over himself to spend time with her? Only why couldn't he just come to Beatrice and tell her he was interested in someone else? Didn't she deserve at least *that* much?

Beatrice trudged across the dead lawn and didn't stop until she reached the woods. She was hurt. And mad. But mostly hurt. She looked down at the bracelet on her arm, remembering how happy she'd been the night Ollie had given it to her. She stood there shivering in the cold for a long time before taking off the bracelet and slipping it into her pocket.

"Well, Cayenne, we're late for Countermagic and Protection," she muttered. "But I'm sure Ollie won't even notice that we're not there."

Cayenne settled like a fur-covered rock against Beatrice's neck and started to purr. It made Beatrice feel a little bit better.

Reaching up to stroke the cat, she said, "You think we'd better get to class? Yeah, I guess you're right."

But just then she heard rustling, and when she turned toward the sound, she saw the fox emerging from the woods. Her red coat glowing in the sunlight, the animal gave Beatrice and Cayenne a long, thoughtful look and then directed her amber eyes toward the school.

Beatrice spent the afternoon in her room, trying to do her homework, but it was hard to concentrate. Finally, she shoved the books off the bed and curled up with Cayenne to take a nap.

She was still wide awake thirty minutes later when she heard a knock on the door, and then Teddy stuck her head in.

"Iris and I are on our way to the kitchen for a snack," Teddy said. "You want to come?"

Beatrice almost said no. But lying in bed feeling sorry for herself wasn't really her style, so she sat up and said, "Sure. I hope Zipporah has some mayfly pie left."

The good news was, there was plenty of pie. The bad news was, Ollie was there, along with Cyrus and Kick, already chowing down on it. When Beatrice walked in and saw Ollie, she was tempted to turn around and go back to her room, but then decided that she had as much right to be there as he did.

Knowing that it was childish, she made a point of sitting as far away from Ollie as possible, and when he cut his eyes at her, she could have sworn that he was mad, too. But what right did *he* have to get huffy? *She* wasn't the one putting on a show for the whole school.

When Zipporah brought the bowl of custard, Cayenne gave an ecstatic cry and rubbed her face against the woman's hand.

"Now, that's what I like to see," Zipporah said, "someone who appreciates my cooking."

"We *all* appreciate your cooking," Cyrus said.

Beatrice was thinking that it was more than Zipporah's mayfly pie that drew them to her. She made them feel at home. And here in this kitchen, among friends, Cyrus was almost his old self again.

Chopping onions at the sink, Zipporah asked over her shoulder, "How are your classes going?"

They all mumbled, "Okay," except for Teddy, who said, "I've learned that I have no magical intuition whatsoever. And since that's what this school is all about, something tells me I won't be here long."

Beatrice wondered why she seemed so cheerful about it. Unless . . .

164

"Teddy," Beatrice said, "did you deliberately goof up on those cards? So they'll send you to another academy—say, Honoria Wagstaffe?"

"I couldn't *deliberately* goof up," Teddy responded, "even if it would get me out of here. It's too humiliating to fail."

"Good thing I don't mind failing," Kick said. "I'd be humiliated all the time."

"But you can predict the future," Cyrus said, "at least, sometimes. All I can do is shrink myself."

There was a crash, and everyone jerked around to see Zipporah staring at a broken ironstone bowl at her feet. Her normally ruddy face was as white as the shards of crockery on the floor, and she seemed to be frozen in place. But then she dropped to her hands and knees and started picking up the pieces, murmuring, "Clumsy, clumsy."

Beatrice and Ollie got up to help her, but Zipporah shooed them away. "Finish your pie," she said. "This won't take a minute."

That's when Beatrice noticed Ollie staring down at her bare wrist, where his bracelet had been for the past three months. She saw a flicker of confusion in his eyes before she turned away and went back to the table.

"Zipporah," Teddy said, "what just happened? It was more than the bowl slipping, wasn't it?"

Zipporah shook her head slightly and continued to pick up the pieces of ironstone. But, after a moment, she sat back on her heels and sighed. Then she got up slowly, dumped the broken crockery into the trash, and came over to the table.

Still pale, she sat down next to Cyrus and said, "I've been keeping a secret and the burden gets heavier every day. Maybe it's time I shared it."

There was a brief silence as she seemed to search for the right words, but then they came bursting out like she'd held them back for too long.

"I want to tell you about Liliana Moonstone. About what happened the last day of her life, and how I failed her." Zipporah was staring past them at nothing, her face a pained mask. "Liliana was such a bright spirit," she said, "but I'd begun to sense that she was troubled about something. I asked her about it, but she wouldn't tell me; she'd just say that everything was fine. Then, early one morning, after Mr. Moonstone had left for the day, she came into the kitchen and told me she was in danger, that she wasn't safe because of something she knew. She said she was leaving Arcana, but that it had to be kept a secret and there wasn't much time."

Zipporah stopped and rubbed her brow wearily. When she looked up, she was less distracted, but the pain was still in her face.

"Liliana told me she couldn't leave right away," Zipporah went on. "She had to go to the bank and run some other errands. But she asked if I'd take Finvarra to a cottage where she'd spent summers with her family growing up. I tried again to get her to tell me why she was so frightened, but she wouldn't. She said, the less I knew, the safer I'd be. So I packed a few things and left with Finvarra."

When Zipporah paused, Ollie said, "That was loyal of you, to help her when you didn't even know what you were getting into."

Zipporah shrugged. "I didn't have any family of my own. Liliana was like a sister to me. And Finvarra—" There was a tremor in her voice and tears suddenly welled in her eyes. "Finvarra was only two, and the sweetest little boy. I loved them and they needed my help. What else could I do?"

"Liliana was going to join you at the cottage?" Teddy asked.

Zipporah nodded. "In the early afternoon. Then the three of us would leave for another part of the Sphere, where no one would be able to find us. Of course, I thought it must be her husband she was afraid of—but, as I said, she wouldn't tell me, and I'd never seen him be anything but kind to her. And he dearly loved his son. *That* bothered me. A rich, powerful man, used to getting his way. What would he do when he came back home and found his boy gone? Well, I tried not to think about that and took Finvarra to the cottage to wait for Liliana. But the afternoon passed and she didn't show up. Then it started to get dark and I couldn't help worrying. So I took Finvarra and went back to the Moonstone estate to look for her. Only no one was there. I didn't know what to do, so I went into the city, thinking I'd check the bank and other places she might have gone. Finvarra and I were approaching the market when it happened."

Zipporah's eyes opened wide, fixed on a spot above Beatrice's head. Her expression was a mixture of disbelief and horror.

"The city started to shake," she said, "and the lights went out. I heard a deafening roar and people screaming. They were running into me, almost knocking me down in their desperation to get away. I'd heard about the monster, of course, and assumed the beast had to be causing this—that it was coming up from the tunnels and meant to kill us all. The city kept shaking and fires broke out. It was terrifying! So I took Finvarra into an alley and waited. For hours, it seemed, till the shaking stopped. But even then, I could hear the cries and moans of people who'd been hurt, who might be dying."

Zipporah let out a long breath. "I was still determined to find Liliana," she said, "so I searched and searched, and several blocks away, I finally saw her. A wall had caved in and she was buried in the rubble. But her face was untouched except for a cut on her forehead, so I recognized her right away. And I could tell she was dead."

"Oh, Zipporah," Beatrice said softly, "I'm so sorry."

All eyes were fixed on the woman's face, except for Cyrus's. He was staring down at his hands.

"But you and Finvarra were all right?" Iris asked.

Zipporah nodded woodenly. "We were fine. He was just frightened, and I knew I had to get him out of there. But I couldn't take him back home, could I? Liliana wanted her son far away from Arcana. So Finvarra and I went back to the cottage, and I sat up the rest of the night, holding him and trying to figure out what to do. I wanted to keep him," she added, her voice cracking, "but I couldn't afford to raise a child on my own, so I— I took him to a children's home a few miles from here and told the matron that he was my child. I gave him a new name—Finn Spitz—and signed custody over to them."

Zipporah was silent for a long time, just gazing into space and giving no indication that she remembered anyone else was there. Then she turned back to them and her eyes locked with Beatrice's.

"I've always felt so guilty," she said, "wondering what happened to that poor little boy after I abandoned him. Yes, that's what I did. I left him with strangers and went back alone to the Moonstone house. I was there when Mr. Moonstone came in, looking terrible. He said the monster had devastated the city, that Liliana was dead, and that Finvarra—along with a lot of other people—was missing, either taken by the monster or buried in the debris. Mr. Moonstone had been out looking for him all night and day. He was grieving for his wife, but it was the loss of his son that obsessed him."

"You never told him what you did?" Beatrice asked gently.

Zipporah shook her head no. "And to this day, I'm not sure if I did the right thing. But I certainly couldn't stay in that house any longer, so I told him it was too sad for me—which was perfectly true—and he arranged with Dr. Cadwallader for me to work here at Widdershins."

They waited for her to go on, but Beatrice had a feeling that she already knew what the woman was going to say next. The pieces were finally beginning to fit together.

"Finvarra had his father's black hair and his mother's brilliant blue eyes," Zipporah said, "and he was such a smart little boy. At two, he could already cast a spell. Do you know what that was?" she asked, looking slowly around the table.

"He could shrink himself," Beatrice said softly.

She heard someone gasp, but her eyes were on Zipporah's face as the woman said, "Yes. He did it all the time, thinking it was hilarious when the rest of us would be frantically looking for him and couldn't find him."

There was complete silence in the room, and now everyone was looking at Cyrus.

He sounded surprisingly calm when he said, "Then you believe that I'm Finvarra Moonstone. That Liliana was my mother."

"I wondered as soon as I saw you," Zipporah said simply. "It was those eyes, Liliana's eyes. And when you said just now that you could shrink yourself . . ." She sighed and added with conviction, "Yes, I do believe you're Liliana's child. You're small like her people, and have their delicate features, too. I'm so sorry," she added in a choked voice. "I should have done better by you. And by your mother."

Cyrus seemed lost in thought and didn't respond.

It was Beatrice who said, "If Cyrus really is the Moonstones' son, that would explain the visions—he was here and actually saw all the chaos."

"And it explains why he can't leave Arcana," Zipporah said. "The monster placed the enchantment over the city after I'd taken him away, so you'd think he wouldn't be affected. But there were other children who were away from the city when the monster cast its spell, and yet, when they returned, they couldn't leave, either. It was decided that the enchantment must affect not only the people who were in Arcana, but also their children and their children's children, for all time. And since Liliana was there, her son was touched by the spell, too."

"But my parents are Silva and Ogden Rascallion," Cyrus murmured. "If I'm adopted, wouldn't they have told me?"

"Maybe not," Ollie said. "They might have thought it best for you not to know."

"Or loved you so much," Teddy said, "they just considered you theirs and didn't think it mattered."

"Are you okay?" Beatrice asked Cyrus.

"Actually," he said, "I'm feeling better than I have in a while. This nightmare is beginning to make sense. But—I need to be sure."

"Of course you do," Ollie said. "We'll figure out a way to prove if you're Liliana's son or not."

"How do we do that?" Teddy asked.

"I have an idea," Beatrice said. "Miranda's doing her fieldwork at the Witches' Institute and that's where they keep official records. She might be able to look at the adoption files."

"Miranda's just a student," Teddy said. "I don't think they'd let her rummage around in private files."

Beatrice smiled. "Have you ever known Miranda to let something as trivial as rules stop her?"

"You have a point," Teddy admitted.

"I'm going upstairs right now to send her a quick-mail," Beatrice said. "I'll see you all at dinner."

"There's just one problem," Kick said suddenly, and they all turned to look at him. "No matter who Cyrus turns out to be, he still can't leave Arcana."

17

What Happened to Milo?

When Beatrice went downstairs with Teddy and Iris for dinner, she saw Ollie outside the dining room with Diantha—*again*— and the sight of them together made her feel hurt and confused and furious, all at the same time.

"Okay, that's it," Teddy said indignantly. "Beatrice, I don't care if you get mad at me or not—it's time you had it out with Ollie. I think he's lost his mind!"

"Probably," Beatrice managed to say, "but that's his problem, isn't it?"

Teddy just stared at her. "Do you *always* have to be so mature about everything?"

But it wasn't maturity that was keeping Beatrice from telling Ollie what she thought of him; it was pride. She didn't want him to know how crushed she was.

The girls sat down with Cyrus and Kick, and at the last minute, Ollie and Diantha came rushing into the dining room. Diantha went to join her friends, and Ollie slid into a chair across from Beatrice. His flushed face and preoccupied expression told her everything she needed to know.

Dinner was awkward. After telling Cyrus that she'd quick-mailed Miranda and asked for her help, Beatrice cut up Cayenne's guppy livers and then ate her own meal in silence. Ollie wasn't talking, either, so Teddy did her best to keep a conversation going.

"This liver's not bad," she remarked.

"Actually, it's pretty good," Kick said.

"A bit slimy," Teddy added, "but the onions help." And then, looking a little desperate, she said into the silence, "I wonder where Cadwallader is. He's not at the faculty table."

"He and Rollo Grubbs go over to Mr. Moonstone's house on Fridays," Kick said. "They have an all-night card game every week."

Still observing the faculty table, Teddy said, "Will you look how Dr. Hawthorn is flirting with Dr. Downs?" But no one seemed interested and she finally gave up.

As soon as dinner was over, Beatrice said, "I think I'll go see if I have a quick-mail from Miranda."

"Um—Beatrice," Ollie said hesitantly, "I'd like to talk to you first. Privately. It won't take long."

Ollie was the last person Beatrice felt like talking to at the moment, but hadn't she wanted him to be honest with her? Well, it looked like he was about to be.

Conscious of everyone at the table watching them, she said curtly, "All right, let's talk."

They left the dining room and went outside. Beatrice had no intention of traipsing all over the grounds in the dark, so she stopped on the steps.

Seeming to sense the tension in the air, Cayenne narrowed her eyes at Ollie and then leaped to her mistress's shoulder, as if declaring whose side she was on.

Beatrice stroked the cat and waited—for Ollie to tell her about Diantha. And then to say that Beatrice had always been such a great friend and he didn't want anything to change that. Beatrice had never had a boyfriend before, so she'd never gone through a breakup, but she'd seen enough movies and TV to know how it worked. Except she really didn't want to hear all that stuff, so why not beat him to the punch?

"Look," she said, staring straight ahead into the darkness, "I know things have changed between us since you met Diantha, and that's okay. There's no reason to make a big deal out of it. I have to tell you, she's not one of *my* favorite people, but you obviously feel differently about her, so—"

"Hold on a minute," Ollie cut in. "I *knew* you thought that, but you've got it all wrong. There's nothing between Diantha and me."

Beatrice's eyes snapped to his face. In the light from the windows, she could see that he was upset. "You aren't—crazy about her?" And when he shook his head emphatically no, she said, "Well, you could've fooled me. Every time I look up, you're running after her."

"I've been going out of my way to talk to her," he admitted, "but only because I was trying to get information."

"What information?" Beatrice asked, knowing she sounded suspicious—because she *was*.

"Remember when Kick said that Milo had it really bad for Diantha?" Ollie asked. "Well, it seemed to me that he never would have gone into the caverns after the monster without telling her. He would have wanted to impress her with how brave he was and with Cadwallader choosing him for a special project."

Beatrice considered this. "Okay, you're probably right," she said.

"So when Diantha acted like she was—well, interested in me," Ollie said, ducking his head slightly, and Beatrice could imagine the color rising in his face, "I decided to spend time with her and see if I could get her to open up about Milo. I was thinking that she might be the only person in the world—besides Cadwallader—who knows what happened to him."

Beatrice was thinking this all made sense, and it sounded exactly like something Ollie would do. But, regardless of his motives, he'd been acting like a jerk!

"So why didn't you tell me this before?" she demanded.

"Because when I suggested that we talk to people," Ollie said, "you were totally against it. Remember? You were afraid Cadwallader would hear about it. But I was so sure Diantha would know something . . . Okay, that's no excuse, I should have told you. But you wouldn't have gone along with it, and we never would have learned anything!"

"So did you learn something?"

Ollie nodded solemnly. "Enough to satisfy me, anyway. You want me to tell you now or should we get everybody together first?"

"Let's go find the others," Beatrice said.

She started for the door, but he touched her arm to stop her. "I hope you believe me," he said. "I could never be interested in Diantha."

Beatrice did believe him, but she couldn't resist saying, "She is very pretty."

"I guess so," Ollie said, "but selfish and spiteful, too. Besides, I thought you and I had—um—an understanding."

The hurt and anger were beginning to dissolve, enough for Beatrice to say, "We do. And maybe I didn't trust you as much as I should have. But from now on, how about trusting me more? I wouldn't have tried to stop you from talking to Diantha, and, anyway, you're free to do anything you want, whether I approve or not."

The worry in Ollie's face had changed to relief. "It's a deal," he said quickly. "And, Beatrice—I hope you'll start wearing the bracelet again. That is—unless you've thrown it away."

"I think you know better than that."

Beatrice reached into the pocket of her sweater for the bracelet, and for the first time all day, she smiled.

A few kids had gathered in the student lounge, including Teddy, Iris, and Kick, who were sitting in what had become "their corner." One look at Beatrice's expression and Teddy grinned. "Is everything okay?" she asked.

"Everything's fine," Beatrice said casually. "Where's Cyrus?"

Kick made a face. "That Harridan woman hauled him off for another one of their sessions."

"Well, Ollie has something to tell us," Beatrice said, "and I don't want to wait till Cyrus gets back. We can fill him in later."

"It's about Milo," Ollie said quietly, and Kick became instantly alert. "Do you think it's safe to talk here?"

"Just keep your voice down," Kick said. "Did you find out what happened to him?"

"Not exactly," Ollie said, "but I'm pretty sure Diantha knows."

"Oh, I get it now," Teddy burst out. "*That's* why you've been hanging around her so much." She gave Ollie a stern look. "I don't mind telling you, I was about to knock some sense into that head of yours."

Ollie sighed. "I know, this hasn't been my finest hour. What I was doing was trying to find out if Milo had told her he was going into the tunnels, only she always managed to change the subject. So tonight, before dinner, I gave it one last shot. I mentioned that I'd heard about a pet project of Cadwallader's that I really wanted to work on, and, *boy*, did that get a reaction. Using language I won't repeat, she told me to forget it. She said . . ." Ollie hesitated and glanced at Kick.

"It's okay," Kick said. "I've figured all along that Milo won't be coming back. Just tell us."

"She said Widdershins had already lost two students because of Cadwallader's ego trip. So I said, 'Yeah, I've heard rumors that a guy named Milo went into the caverns last year and never came back.' Well, she looked totally shocked, and then she said, 'But I'm the only one'—and caught herself. But I'm pretty sure she was about to say that she was the only one who knew that—besides Cadwallader, of course."

Kick was nodding slowly. "I think you're right."

"Did Diantha tell you anything else?" Beatrice asked.

"Not about Milo," Ollie said. "I kept pressing, but she clammed up. You know, that was the first time I'd seen her act nervous—maybe even a little scared. But the only thing she said after that was, 'If you know what's good for you, you won't mention this project or Milo to anyone else. Believe me, you don't want it getting back to Cadwallader.' Oh, and she said if I told anyone I'd talked to her about it, she'd deny it."

"Well, it seems pretty certain that Milo and Sadie did go into the tunnels," Teddy said.

"And when they didn't come back," Iris added, "Cadwallader tried to cover it up with that story of them running off together."

"I guess that's why he's so determined to pick what he calls the *right people* next time," Ollie said. "He'd have a hard time explaining the disappearance of more students."

"I just thought of something," Beatrice said suddenly. "You know how Diantha sleeps through class and never does any homework? I'll bet she told Cadwallader what she knows and he agreed to let her graduate whether she does any work or not, as long as she keeps her mouth shut about Milo and Sadie."

"You mean she's blackmailing him?" Teddy asked.

"It makes sense," Ollie said. "That's why she got so nervous when I mentioned Milo disappearing. If Cadwallader got the idea that she'd talked, she might lose her free ride."

"Or worse," Beatrice murmured. "She's probably scared of him, and with good reason."

Kick had been chewing on his lip and staring at the floor, but now he looked up and said quietly, "It won't bring Milo and Sadie back, but I'm going after Bane."

Beatrice blew her bangs out of her eyes and said, "Well, you sure as heck aren't going alone."

18

Into the Woods

"Whaen would we go?" Ollie asked.

Kick said, "What's wrong with tonight? Cadwallader won't be back from Mr. Moonstone's till dawn, so we can go to his office and get the sword and sleeping powders without him catching us."

"Run this by me again," Teddy said, frowning. "Why is it exactly that we want to go after the monster and get ourselves killed?"

"*I'm* going because of Milo," Kick said. "I owe him that much. Cadwallader doesn't care what happened to him, but I do."

"Okay, I can understand that," Teddy said more gently. "But, Kick, if your friend couldn't succeed after all that careful planning, what makes you think we can? And another thing. I don't mean to sound cold-hearted—and I do feel really bad about Milo—but we didn't even know him."

"That's true," Kick said, looking at her steadily, "but you know Cyrus. And the only way he's ever going to get out of this city is if the monster is destroyed. They say the enchantment would die with it."

"But we don't have a plan," Beatrice said. "And I don't have the headmaster's confidence that magical intuition will get us through this. Why can't we wait and give ourselves time to work it out?"

"I would agree with you," Ollie said, "except for one thing. I did make it unsafe for us, talking to Diantha. What if she decides to tell Cadwallader that I've been snooping around about Milo? She might think she'd come off looking better if he heard it from her first."

"That could be a problem," Teddy agreed. "He might send us home, and then Cyrus would be stuck here by himself."

"You know," Iris said, blinking rapidly, "I don't want to—to seem like a coward, but I'm not quite ready to—face a monster."

"That's okay," Ollie said. "All of us shouldn't go, anyway. Someone has to be here who knows what we're doing, just in case . . ."

"And Cyrus shouldn't go," Beatrice said. "He's been through too much lately."

"Okay," Teddy said. "It's just the four of us then."

"So you want to go?" Beatrice asked.

"Not especially," Teddy admitted. "But I want to get Cyrus out of this place. And we did tell Kick we'd help if Cadwallader picked us for the project. We're just not waiting for our official assignment, that's all."

"Okay, then," Beatrice said to Kick, "tell us everything Milo told you."

Late that night, after everyone else was asleep, Beatrice crept down the stairs with Cayenne on her shoulder and Teddy beside her. They were wearing running shoes and heavy jackets and had flashlights in their pockets.

The academy was quiet except for the faint moans and shrieks coming from one of the upper floors—but Beatrice was pretty sure that was just Rhude and Rankin doing more of their clumsy haunting. Moonlight streamed through the windows, allowing them to find their way to Dr. Cadwallader's office, where Ollie and Kick were waiting.

Ollie tried the door and it creaked open. Once Beatrice, Teddy, and Kick had followed him inside, he shut it as quietly as he could and then turned on his flashlight.

"The sleeping potion is hidden inside a book," Kick whispered as they went into the inner office. "It's called *The Sleeping Giant*. I remember that because Milo thought it was funny."

Beatrice, Teddy, and Kick switched on their flashlights and started to scan the bookshelves. When Ollie had the sword, he came to help them.

There were a lot of books to check, but finally Beatrice said, "Here it is," and pulled a thick volume off the shelf.

It was hollow inside and contained several small glass vials of white powder. Kick reached for one and stuck it into his pocket.

"Okay," he said, "we have the sleeping potion and the sword. Now all we need is some raw meat."

They turned off their flashlights, left the office, and started down a narrow back hall. As they were approaching the kitchen door, Teddy whispered, "What's that noise?"

Beatrice stopped to listen. She could hear murmurs and faint, tinkling laughter. "I think it's coming from the kitchen," she said softly.

Teddy pushed gently on the door and light spilled out into the hall. Instantly, the voices ceased. Beatrice peeked in and saw at least a dozen tiny creatures, all wearing brightly colored caps and kerchiefs, scattered across the room. They had been sweeping up crumbs with miniature brooms and washing plates as large as themselves—but now they stood as motionless as statues, their startled eyes trained on the door.

It was the Ellyons who helped Zipporah, and Beatrice remembered that they didn't like being seen. But before she could apologize for disturbing them, the elves suddenly sprang to life, leaping off counters and tossing their brooms aside, all the while chattering in high, thin voices that were decidedly agitated. Then the back door swung open and the creatures skittered out into the night.

"Uh-oh," Beatrice said. "I think Zipporah's going to be running another ad in *The Elf Examiner*."

Teddy snickered as she opened the door to the freezer. Inside were shelves piled high with raw meat wrapped in clear plastic.

Beatrice stared dubiously at the freezer's contents. "This doesn't look like beef—or anything else I've ever seen. What do you suppose it is?"

"We probably don't want to know," Ollie answered.

"This stuff isn't going to thaw for hours," Teddy said. "I hope the monster can smell frozen meat."

A few minutes later, Kick lifted a pillowcase filled with meat to his shoulder. As they were leaving through the back door, Beatrice whispered to him, "We haven't talked about the sky dancers. Can they really stop us?"

"Oh, they can stop us all right," Kick answered softly. "Cadwallader was going to give them instructions to let Milo and his team pass, but we'll just have to take our chances. I've been watching them, and I've noticed that they mostly patrol the front campus and don't go into the woods. So all we have to do is make it across the lawn to the trees." He pulled a collapsible telescope out of his jacket and gave it to Beatrice. "We can pretend to be looking at the stars till the sky dancers go away. Then we'll take off for the woods."

Beatrice looked down at Cayenne, who was sitting at her feet, and said, "You'd better not come this time, Cay. We don't know what we're getting into. So go back to bed and I'll see you later."

Whereupon, Cayenne proceeded to saunter out the door.

"Cayenne!" Beatrice said sharply.

185

"She's always gone with us before," Teddy pointed out. "She'll be okay."

In any case, it was too late to stop the cat now; she was already dashing across the lawn. The rest of them followed, trying to look casual—which wasn't easy with Ollie hiding a sword inside his jacket and Kick carrying a heavy bag of frozen meat over his shoulder.

"Where's the best place to set up the telescope?" Kick asked in a loud voice.

"Over there would be good," Beatrice answered in ringing tones.

Since they were supposed to be looking at stars, and trees would block the sky, they had to stay near the center of the lawn. But when Kick selected a spot about twenty yards away from the woods, Beatrice started to worry. She had no idea what the sky dancers might do to them, but she knew they were fast, and that seemed like a long distance to have to cover.

Kick put down his sack and took the telescope from Beatrice. Meanwhile, the sky dancers were starting to gather overhead, the moonlight catching their filmy wings and turning them silver.

"This was such a good idea," Teddy shouted. "I just *love* astronomy."

Looking up at the sky, Beatrice called out, "There's the Big Dipper," while she watched more sky dancers arrive. There had to be at least twenty of them now, all darting around and keeping a close eye on Beatrice and her friends.

And then another voice rang out.

"What are you guys doing?"

They all turned around to see Cyrus loping across the lawn toward them.

Beatrice met him halfway. "I thought you were in bed," she said softly.

"I couldn't sleep," Cyrus answered, lowering his voice to match hers, "and I happened to look out the window and see you all. So what are you doing?"

"We're looking at the stars," Beatrice said, glancing up at the sky dancers still circling overhead.

As Cyrus walked over to investigate the telescope, she was wondering how they were going to get him to go back inside.

"Um—hi, Cyrus," Ollie said.

"Why didn't you come get me?" Cyrus asked. "You know I like looking at the constellations."

"Well—we—um—thought you'd be asleep," Teddy stammered, "and—we didn't want to disturb you."

There was a moment's silence, then Cyrus said, "What's really going on? You're up to something."

"Keep your voices down," Kick hissed at them.

"Tell me what you're doing," Cyrus whispered, "and I'll be quiet."

Ollie glanced at Beatrice, shrugged, and then told Cyrus everything.

"And you were trying to sneak off without me knowing," Cyrus said, as if he couldn't believe it. "But we've always faced danger together, as a team. And if you're going down into—"

"*Hush!*" Kick warned them urgently under his breath and jerked his head in the direction of the sky dancers.

"If you're going into the tunnels," Cyrus said, in a whisper this time, "then I should be there. I have more at stake here than any of you. And if you're worried that I'm going to crack up, I won't. Honest."

"He's right," Beatrice said. "He *does* have a lot at stake."

"And I promise I won't slow you down," Cyrus added.

After some whispered discussion, they agreed that Cyrus would go with them.

"The stargazing is just a cover, to put the sky dancers off track," Kick told him. "When I give the word, run as fast as you can into the woods and don't stop for anything."

They took turns looking through the telescope, which Beatrice might have enjoyed if she hadn't been so jumpy. But Cyrus's unexpected appearance had just given her something else to worry about.

Eventually, the sky dancers started drifting toward the front of the academy. When the last two flew off, Kick whispered, "Okay, on the count of three, start running."

Beatrice scooped up Cayenne and tucked the cat into the front of her jacket.

"One," Kick said. "Two. *Three.*"

Beatrice took off. Feet pounding against the frozen ground, she didn't look back, even when she heard a sky dancer bellow, "Stay out of the woods! I repeat. *Stay out of the woods!*

It wasn't until she'd entered the trees that Beatrice glanced around. Cyrus and Ollie were on either side of her and Kick was just behind them. But where was Teddy?

They all came to a stop and looked back across the moon-drenched lawn. And there she was, standing perfectly still, maybe ten yards from the woods. Bewildered, Beatrice wondered why Teddy wasn't running. But then she saw two sky dancers flying in tight circles around Teddy—binding her with what looked like shimmery, silver thread.

"Oh, great," Kick muttered. "That's fairy rope. Strong as steel. It's one of the ways the sky dancers keep us here. But don't worry, they won't hurt her."

Beatrice wasn't sure of that at all. Especially when, wrapped from chin to ankles in fairy rope, Teddy toppled to the ground like a falling tree.

19

Under the City

Beatrice's first instinct was to go back and help Teddy. She started toward the lawn, but Kick grabbed her arm.

"She's okay," he said, "and you couldn't cut through that rope, anyway. We'll see about her when we get back."

"And if we don't get back?" Beatrice asked.

"Then someone will find her when the sun comes up," Kick said reasonably, "and Cadwallader will tell the sky dancers to release her."

Still torn, Beatrice called out, "Teddy, are you all right?"

"I—think so," came the faint reply. "No bones broken. I know you have to go—just don't be too long, okay? And be careful!"

Beatrice didn't like the idea of leaving Teddy trapped and defenseless, but she didn't see that they had much choice. "We'll be back as soon as we can," Beatrice called to her.

"They must have heard you," Ollie said. He was pointing through the trees at a squad of sky dancers speeding toward them, their gauzy wings glimmering in the moonlight.

"I don't *think* they'll come into the woods," Kick said, "but we'd better get moving."

"There's a path around here somewhere," Beatrice said.

But Kick had already started running again, and the others took off after him. Before long, they found themselves in a thick tangle of trees and underbrush and had to slow down. A dog was barking nearby and they heard a growl that might have come from a wild cat. Cayenne poked her head out of Beatrice's jacket and turned her ears toward the sounds.

Ollie said, "We must be close to the animal preserve."

"And we have to be careful," Beatrice said. "If Cyrus steps outside the city, he'll be frozen."

"Okay, we can turn north and stay on school grounds till we reach the street," Kick said. "Come on."

Once they'd changed course, the animal sounds gradually faded away. The dense growth of trees shut out most of the moonlight and they had to feel their way along in the darkness, still managing to trip over roots and get caught on thorny bushes. Then, all of a sudden, Beatrice saw a light shining through the branches.

"Is that the city?" she asked.

"No, I think it's Moonstone's house," Kick said.

Beatrice kept her eye on the light as they walked, making sure they didn't come too close to it. Finally, the trees thinned enough for her to see the outline of a large stone house. The light was coming from one of the downstairs windows.

They continued on through the woods until the Moonstone house was behind them. And before long, they saw a streetlight up ahead, then light spilling onto pavement.

When they reached the sidewalk, Cyrus asked, "How much farther?"

"A couple of blocks," Kick said.

They took off down the street, where there were no cars, no people, no signs of life anywhere—just eerie silence all around them. At night, Arcana turned into a true ghost town.

"Well, there it is," Kick said, and came to a stop.

In front of them was a concrete wall with a wide opening in the center. Beatrice thought it could have been a subway entrance in the mortal world; but here, in Arcana, it was the doorway to a monster's lair.

The silence stretched out as they stood there looking at the black, gaping hole. A knot of fear tightened in Beatrice's stomach and she could see the tension in her friends' faces.

Kick lowered the sack of meat to the sidewalk and said softly, "All right, I guess it's time."

He reached into his pocket for the sleeping potion and Ollie drew the sword from inside his jacket. Beatrice pulled slabs of meat from the pillowcase and began to tear off the plastic wrapping.

"Still solid as a rock," she murmured.

"Let's just hope Bane has a strong sense of smell," Kick said.

He sprinkled sleeping potion on the meat and they carried it into the tunnel, placing it on the concrete floor just inside the entrance. It was too dark to see much of anything, but Beatrice could feel the tunnel sloping downward, and a nasty, rotting smell reached her nostrils.

"Let's get out of here," Ollie whispered.

Once out of the tunnel, they crouched down at the side of the entrance and waited. A long time passed and nothing happened. Cayenne grew restless and crawled out of Beatrice's jacket, but Beatrice caught her and tucked her back inside.

"I don't understand it," Kick whispered. "Milo said the monster was supposed to come right away for its food."

"Maybe we need to carry it deeper into the tunnel," Cyrus said.

"I guess we'd be able to tell if the thing was coming," Beatrice said. "From everything I've heard, it isn't exactly light on its feet."

"And at the first sound," Kick said, "we drop the meat and run."

They entered the tunnel, put the meat back into the pillowcase, and Kick lifted it to his shoulder. Then they turned on their flashlights and started down the wide passageway. It wasn't long before the concrete ended and Beatrice could see that the tunnel was carved out of solid rock. As they made their descent deeper and deeper into the earth, the stench grew worse and the air turned colder. Beatrice had to clench her teeth to keep them from chattering.

Ollie was walking beside her, moving his flashlight beam back and forth across the tunnel floor, the sword held out in front of him. Kick and Cyrus were on either side of them. There was only the faint sound their shoes made against the stone to break the silence.

The ground had finally begun to level off when Cyrus said in a low voice, "Look, more tunnels."

Just ahead were several passageways branching off from the main one.

"We keep going straight," Kick said.

They continued down the tunnel, listening intently for any sound, until finally it opened into a cavern that was so vast their flashlight beams were lost in the dark enormity of it. But Beatrice could see that the path they were on ended a few feet ahead—at the edge of a huge black hole.

"Watch out," she said quickly, forgetting to be quiet. "We don't want to fall into—*that*."

"Wow," Kick said. He took a few steps and leaned over to peer into the crater. "This must be about the size of Lake Superior." He aimed his flashlight into it and added, "I can't see the bottom—if it has one."

Meanwhile, Ollie was shining his light along the edge of the hole. "There's solid rock around it—at least, as far as I can see. Which way do we go?"

But he never got an answer. Because, at that moment, the cavern started to shake. Beatrice could feel the stone floor vibrating under her feet, sending tremors up her legs and body. Then came a blast of sound—a roar so loud and terrible, she instinctively cried out and covered her ears. In the chaotic moments that followed, Beatrice lost her footing and tumbled to the ground. She saw the sword go flying into the air—right before Ollie fell beside her. Out of the corner of her eye, she caught sight of Cyrus, still clutching his flashlight and holding on to an outcrop of rock, and Kick on his hands and knees, trying to stand up.

Ollie reached out to Beatrice. She saw his lips moving, but she couldn't hear what he was saying over that earsplitting noise. All she could do was squeeze his hand and hold on to the trembling cat inside her jacket.

Then Ollie was pointing to the side of the tunnel, where Cyrus was hanging on for dear life. Beatrice realized that he meant for them to try to make it over there, and it seemed like a good idea—to get as far away from the hole as possible. She nodded that she understood.

While Beatrice watched, Ollie got to his knees and started to crawl away from her. She realized now that she was only three or four feet away from the edge of the crater. *Close call*, she was thinking. And that's when it happened.

In the beam of Cyrus's flashlight, Beatrice saw an enormous black shape begin to rise up out of the hole. She knew instantly that she was about to come face-to-face with Bane—but was too shaken by the vibrations and thunderous noise to think about being afraid.

Keeping one hand on Cayenne, she started edging back from the hole, but that monstrous thing had reared up into the air, its shadow already falling over her. Even as she inched away, she couldn't take her eyes off it. There was the outline of a head—and jaws opening slowly—massive, *terrifying* jaws! And Beatrice found herself staring into a mouth that was at least ten feet wide.

She knew it was too late to save herself, but there was one thing she could do. Swaying unsteadily on her knees, she lifted Cayenne out of her jacket and dropped the cat to the ground.

"Run, Cayenne!" Beatrice screamed, as the gaping mouth came down to claim her.

20

Fox Fire

*A*nd then, just as she expected those deadly jaws to close around her, something came sailing through the air and struck Beatrice's back—knocking her flat. Her chin came down hard on the rough stone floor, sending a jolt of pain up her face to the top of her skull. She lay there half stunned as those jaws snapped shut only inches above her prone body.

The monster!

Head spinning, Beatrice couldn't quite comprehend what had happened. Then something soft and warm pressed against her neck, and she realized it was Cayenne—that it must have been Cayenne who slammed into her, pushing her clear of the monster's gaping mouth.

The monster!

Beatrice rolled onto her back and there it was, that enormous black shape, hovering over her. But then, all of a sudden, it seemed to draw back—and was she just imagining it, or was the beast sinking back into its hole?

The cavern was still shaking, the roar vibrating off the rock walls—and that was when Beatrice realized that something was wrong. The monster *was* sinking

197

into the crater—with its mouth *closed!* So where was the roar coming from?

Just then, Beatrice saw Ollie crawling toward her, clutching his flashlight. By the time he reached her, the monster had disappeared into the pit. Beatrice's one aim was to get the heck out of there, so she couldn't believe what Ollie did next. He actually crawled to the edge of the hole and shone a beam down into it. Beatrice saw a startled look flash across his face. Then he motioned for them to join him.

They crept forward and aimed their own flashlights into the crater. And there it was! The monster was resting just below the lip of rock where they were crouched. It lay perfectly still. And it was—*shiny*, like a black car with a really good paint job. That was when it dawned on Beatrice that the creature wasn't even *alive*. It was made out of metal!

Her eyes darted to the boys' faces. One look and she knew that they, too, had realized the truth. This thing wasn't a monster; it was a machine made to *look* like a monster. And it must be activated by sound or light or something—to rise up and scare people senseless!

The shaking was causing bits of rock to fall from the walls and ceiling of the cavern. Glancing back to see if the tunnel was still clear, Beatrice's eyes fell on a hollowed-out space near the cavern's entrance. She aimed her light that way and saw that it was another cave, small compared to the one they were in, but at least thirty feet wide. And it was crammed full of machinery—giant mechanical hammers pounding steel plates, each strike of metal against metal causing the rock around them to shudder. And in the corner was a huge gray box with giant speakers on top. *That* was where the roar was coming from. It was a recording!

The boys were staring in astonishment, and then Ollie mouthed the words, "It's a hoax!"

That was when Cyrus pointed to the far corner of the cave. There were huge piles of—what? Beatrice strained to see and then wished she hadn't. Slabs of rotting meat were stacked up nearly to the ceiling. So this was what happened to the monster's food. Someone hid the meat here so that it would seem as if Bane had eaten it. Well, at least they knew where that terrible stench was coming from.

Beatrice didn't understand exactly what she was seeing, but she thought it best for them to try to make sense of it aboveground. Only how were they going to get out of here when they couldn't even stand up? Maybe, if they could manage to crawl out of the cavern and back into the tunnel, the vibrations would be less intense away from the hammering.

She was trying to get to her knees when she noticed Cayenne huddled against her, obviously terrified by the noise and shaking. But frightened or not, the cat had risked her life in order to shove Beatrice away from those monstrous jaws. And even if they were made of metal instead of flesh and bone, they would have crushed the life out of her if Cayenne hadn't come to her rescue.

Beatrice picked up the trembling cat and held her close before tucking her back inside her jacket. But about that time the mechanical monster rose up from the crater again, and they all skittered on hands and knees toward the cavern entrance. Once she was far enough away to feel safe, Beatrice looked back over her shoulder. The monster was opening its mouth, seeming to roar in fury at them. But when Beatrice shone her light on the jaws, she could see bolted hinges and jagged, metal teeth.

She turned back toward the tunnel, and that's when she felt a hand grasp her arm. Twisting around, she saw Kick's alarmed face—then him pointing to the side of the crater, where, suddenly, the blackness was illuminated by a dozen or more flickering lights. Torches, Beatrice realized, being carried by figures in dark robes that had appeared out of nowhere and were skirting the edge of the pit.

It was the men from the bus who'd tried to kidnap her! Only there were lots more now—twenty, at least— all moving swiftly toward Beatrice and her friends.

She still had no idea who they were, but it was obvious that they weren't coming to help. And Ollie must have been thinking the same thing because now he was the one gesturing—urgently—toward the tunnel. It was only a few yards away, but getting there on their hands and knees would take time. Then Beatrice realized that the closer the torch guys came to the hammers, the more trouble they were having staying on their feet. One of them fell, then another. Still peering back over her shoulder, Beatrice was crawling as fast as she could alongside the boys when she saw one of their pursuers point directly at the machine-filled cave. And instantly, the shaking and roaring stopped.

Beatrice's head was throbbing and she was feeling disoriented. She didn't quite know what was happening when Ollie and Cyrus jerked her to her feet. But with an instinct for survival, she started running.

They sped out of the cavern and up the slope of the tunnel. Even without looking back, Beatrice could tell that their pursuers were close behind. She could hear the slapping of hard soles against stone, and the torchlight seemed to grow brighter as the hooded figures gained on them.

Beatrice kept going, but running uphill wasn't easy. Her legs were getting tired and her breath was coming in shallow pants. And they still had a long way to the top.

But they couldn't give up! They had to make it out of here and tell everyone that the monster didn't exist—that something even worse seemed to be going on. Beatrice was thinking that she couldn't die without figuring all this out when Kick stumbled and fell to the ground.

While Ollie and Cyrus helped him up, Beatrice jerked her head around and saw that their pursuers weren't more than a hundred feet away. Her heart sank as she realized the futility of trying to outrun them. But Ollie was pulling on her hand, and Beatrice started running again.

And that's when she saw it—a flash of red speeding down the tunnel toward them. It was the fox!

The animal darted past them, and Beatrice and her friends spun around, watching as the creature ran a few more feet—then came to an abrupt halt. As the torches and trampling feet moved closer, the fox sat down and began to beat her bushy tail on the rock. And, suddenly, flames were leaping up from the floor of the tunnel.

The fox jumped clear and trotted back toward Beatrice and her companions, who were staring in amazement as the fire grew into a blazing wall. They could no longer see the dark figures through the flames, but they could hear angry, frustrated cries. Because the chase was over.

And there stood the fox a few feet away, her coat glowing as brightly as the fire, regarding them calmly with her soft amber eyes. No, not *them*, Beatrice corrected herself. The fox spirit was looking directly at Cyrus.

That was when the bits and pieces began to fall into place. Beatrice thought she finally knew why the fox had come to help them. And from the faintly astonished smile on Cyrus's face, Beatrice realized that he'd figured it out, too.

21

One Piece Missing

They were nearing the top of the tunnel when Beatrice began to hear faint shouts and cries. By the time they emerged onto the street, the voices had become a din of fear and anguish. All around them, people were running, clutching babies and small children, crying, screaming for help. A building near the tunnel entrance had collapsed, leaving only piles of brick and roofing heaped across the pavement, and in the next block, flames were glowing against the night sky.

Beatrice was vaguely aware of the fox sprinting past her and disappearing down an alley, but she was too shocked by the sight of all this devastation to give the animal much thought. Then she remembered Cyrus and turned anxiously to see how he was reacting. His eyes were huge and filled with horror as they took in the chaos around him, and Beatrice wondered if he was reliving a time eleven years ago when he'd witnessed a scene just like this one. She reached for his hand and he seemed to snap back to the present.

"These people are terrified," he said. "Can't we tell them there's no monster?"

"Most of them are hysterical," Ollie replied, his expression somber as he watched a sobbing woman pulling two children down the street. "I don't think they'd hear us."

"Well, we'd better get back to the academy and tell—*someone*," Kick said. "I'm just not sure who we can trust."

"We'll try to figure that out on the way," Beatrice said.

They didn't speak again until they reached the Moonstone house and stopped to catch their breath. Through the trees, they could see that most of the first floor of the mansion was lit up now, but the house was silent.

"Well, that's one card game that broke up early," Kick said. "They'd have felt the tremors and gone to investigate, don't you think?"

"Maybe they're the ones behind all this," Cyrus said darkly.

"But why?" Beatrice asked. "Okay, let's think this through. What do we know for sure?"

"We know the monster doesn't exist," Ollie said, "but someone wants people to *think* it does. And we know that those guys with the torches were after us—and I'm pretty sure they meant business."

"They probably went after Milo and Sadie, too," Kick said angrily, "and all the other witches who've disappeared over the last decade."

"But why?" Ollie asked. "And who can help us get to the bottom of this?"

"Not the mayor," Beatrice said. "Remember that night at dinner when he told us he'd seen the monster on the street?"

"That's right!" Ollie exclaimed. "But he *couldn't* have."

"He must know the monster's a fake," Cyrus said.

"And he still takes money from the people of Arcana to feed it," Beatrice said. "There was an awful lot of meat down there, but he might be able to skim off enough cash to keep some for himself."

"That's it," Kick said eagerly. "Rollo Grubbs came up with the idea of the monster just so he could make some extra money. And I'll bet anything Cadwallader's in on it with him."

"Maybe . . .," Ollie said thoughtfully. "But how would Cadwallader benefit from it? I think he'd want a *real* monster—so he can prove his theory. Of course, he couldn't care less if his students *die* trying to prove it— so he's not exactly a nice guy—but he believes totally in the concept of magical intuition and I think he'd want it to be a legitimate challenge."

"That makes sense," Kick admitted. "So the mayor's doing this on his own? Or do you think Moonstone's involved, too?"

"I don't see how Mr. Moonstone would benefit, either," Ollie said. "He's already rich, and the little bit Rollo Grubbs could squeeze out of people would be pocket change to Moonstone."

"And, anyway," Beatrice said, "he seems to care more about his animals than money."

"So what do we do?" Cyrus asked. "Go back to school and tell Cadwallader everything we know?"

"I guess," Kick said. "But he and the mayor are pretty tight. I wonder if he'll believe us."

"We'll *make* him believe us," Beatrice said. "Come on, we have to help Teddy, too. I'll bet she's furious."

When they finally emerged from the woods, they saw that most of the lights in the school were on.

"Uh-oh," Cyrus muttered. "I think we're in trouble."

"We'll worry about that later," Beatrice said. "Right now, we have to see about Teddy."

But Teddy wasn't there. When they went over to the spot where she'd been lying, all that remained was a silvery tangle of fairy rope.

"She's already been released," Beatrice said. "Well, that's good. But I'll bet they've been giving her the third degree."

"I wouldn't doubt it," came a voice from the woods, and then Cormac stepped out.

"I got your friend loose," he said, "but that Harridan woman came out screeching like a bat and dragged her inside. They've had the sky dancers searching the grounds for the rest of you."

"Poor Teddy," Beatrice murmured.

"Poor *us*," Cyrus said.

Beatrice knew they'd all be in hot water, but she couldn't help smiling. Because Cyrus was acting so *normal*. And after everything he'd been through tonight. She'd noticed him looking around as they walked back through the woods, and she thought he was probably hoping to catch a glimpse of the fox. As a matter of fact, she wouldn't mind seeing that old fox spirit again herself. But right now, they had to go inside and try to get Cadwallader to listen to them.

Mrs. Harridan and Toogood Mars were waiting for them in the front hall. All the other students must have been sent to bed, but the teachers were hanging over the second-floor railing, watching. As soon as she saw Beatrice and her friends, Mrs. Harridan started raging, pacing back and forth in her pink robe.

"What gall!" she screeched. "You've been nothing but trouble since you arrived. And now *this!* Sneaking off campus in the middle of the night! Oh, I told Dr. Cadwallader he should send you all packing." Then her eyes fell on Cyrus and she was momentarily silenced, obviously realizing that they'd *tried* to send him packing and couldn't. But it didn't take long for her to pick up speed again. "Well, if I have anything to say about it, every one of you will be expelled. And that goes for you, too, Mr. Tazwell. I always said it was a mistake to take students from the mortal world."

While she went on ranting and pacing, Toogood Mars just stood there glaring at them. But then there was a shriek and Teddy came barreling down the stairs, beaming. Wearing her pajamas and robe, she looked none the worse for her encounter with the sky dancers.

"I'm so glad to see you," Teddy said, hugging them all. Then she whispered, "I didn't admit anything, but they know you left campus."

207

"*Miss Berry*, what did I tell you?" Mrs. Harridan screamed. "You were to stay in your room. I still have *some* authority around here."

"That's enough, Mrs. Harridan," came a deep, quiet voice from the doorway behind them.

Beatrice turned around to face Dr. Cadwallader and saw the barely-controlled fury in his eyes.

"I want to see all five of you in my office," he said, "*now*. Mrs. Harridan, I won't be needing you again tonight."

Beatrice saw the woman's face fall in disappointment, then flush with renewed anger.

"Step to it, Miss Bailiwick," the headmaster snapped.

It was like being marched down the hall to their executions. *But surely*, Beatrice thought, *once he hears that there's no monster—and that the mayor is fully aware of that . . .*

There was just one problem, which they all recognized as soon as they stepped into Dr. Cadwallader's inner office. Mr. Moonstone and the mayor were already there.

The two men stared at Beatrice and her friends as they entered. Rollo Grubbs appeared nervous, Januarius Moonstone merely curious.

Dr. Cadwallader sat down behind his desk and looked up at Beatrice, eyes blazing behind his glasses. "Your behavior is unacceptable," he said, his face stony and ungiving. "I had high hopes for all of you, but I see now that my trust was misplaced. So tell me, just where were you tonight?"

But then Rollo Grubbs sat forward in his chair and said quickly, "Don't be too hard on them, Hodge. We were all young once, and didn't always use the best judgment. It's been a terrible night—what with Bane surfacing again—and, wherever they were, I'm sure the commotion scared them to death. So why not send them off to bed, and then you can all talk sensibly about this in the morning?"

Appearing vaguely bored, Mr. Moonstone said, "Good idea, Rollo. They must be exhausted."

"And I have something to discuss with you, Hodge," the mayor cut in anxiously. "It really can't wait."

Beatrice had been watching Mr. Moonstone and now she saw that Cyrus was, too. *What must Cyrus be thinking,* she wondered, *being this close to the man who might be his biological father?* But Cyrus's face was carefully composed and she had no idea what was going on inside his head.

For a moment, no one spoke. Then Dr. Cadwallader said, "All right, we'll wait till morning to talk about this." He was obviously still livid as his gaze fell on Beatrice and the others. "But you're all to go directly to your rooms—and *stay there* until you're called. Is that clear?"

"Yes, sir," they said in unison, and then hurried out of the office before he could change his mind.

They had just passed the dining room when Kick said softly, "Let's duck into the lounge. We have to talk."

Leaving the door open for light, they headed for their corner.

"So tell me what happened," Teddy said impatiently. "Did you see the monster?"

"There is no monster," Ollie said, and quickly filled her in.

"This is unbelievable," Teddy said. "Not only has someone been terrorizing Arcana with a made-up monster, but he must have placed the enchantment over the city, too. Why would the mayor do that?"

"Well, if everyone left," Kick answered, "who would pay him to keep the monster quiet?"

"Did you notice," Beatrice said suddenly, "how nervous Mr. Grubbs was? He didn't want Cadwallader questioning us."

"I thought the same thing," Ollie said. "So Cadwallader *must* not know the monster's a fake, and the mayor didn't want us telling him. The guys that came after us have probably already told Grubbs what we saw."

"But what's the difference between us talking to Cadwallader tonight or in the morning?" Beatrice mused.

"Maybe Grubbs wants to tell him first," Ollie said.

"You mean before he shuts us up permanently?" Teddy asked.

"Yeah, we know too much, don't we?" Beatrice said. "Except . . . it isn't adding up. Rollo Grubbs couldn't be making much money off this. After he's paid the guys with the torches, how much could he have left? And besides, would he actually kill people—and lots of people, it appears—for so little profit?"

"You're right," Ollie said. "There's a piece missing."

"So what do we do now?" Teddy asked. "We can't be sure who's been running this monster scam—or why—and we're probably in danger."

"You all have to leave Arcana," Cyrus said firmly. "Get out of here as fast as you can."

Beatrice was about to protest that she had no intention of leaving without him when Ollie suddenly hushed them and said, "Listen."

They heard scuffling out in the hall, and then Dr. Cadwallader saying in an angry voice, "I won't be a party to this. Let *go* of me!"

Beatrice and her friends crept to the doorway and peered cautiously around the frame. What they saw were Rollo Grubbs and Januarius Moonstone pulling a resisting Cadwallader down the corridor toward the front of the house. Then Moonstone placed a hand on the headmaster's shoulder and mumbled something. Instantly, Cadwallader's body relaxed and he stopped fighting.

Completely docile now, his face as blank as a zombie's, the headmaster continued down the hall between his two captors.

22

A Noble Cause?

They heard the front door open, then close.

"Come on," Ollie said.

Running through the front hall, which was now deserted, and out the door, they saw the men disappear around the side of the building.

"They're probably taking him to Moonstone's house," Kick whispered. "I'll bet Cadwallader's about to vanish like all those other witches."

"We have to do something," Teddy said.

Seeming to agree, Cayenne took off after the men, with Beatrice and her friends close behind. As they came around the corner, they saw the trio heading for the woods.

"Okay, now what?" Cyrus asked.

In desperation, Beatrice began to chant:

Circle of magic, hear my pleas,
Send lightning down
On our enemies.
This, I ask you, do for me.

All at once, thunder rumbled, then exploded overhead. Startled, Moonstone and Grubbs stopped short, just as a jagged bolt of lightning shot down from the sky and struck—only inches from their feet. The two men jumped back, pulling their catatonic prisoner with them. But the spears of lightning followed them, striking first to their left, then to their right—until, suddenly, Rollo Grubbs let out a terrified cry and started running for the nearest tree.

"Bad move," Cyrus murmured. "Doesn't lightning strike trees?"

They watched as the mayor tried frantically to shinny up the trunk, breaking small limbs that couldn't bear his weight and scraping off bark with his shoes.

Januarius Moonstone was screaming, "You idiot! Come down from there!"

When the desperate mayor ignored him, Moonstone let go of the headmaster and stalked over to the tree. He grabbed hold of Rollo Grubbs's robes, and still shouting insults, tried to pull him down. Meanwhile, Cadwallader seemed to be waking up from his dream state and was looking around in confusion.

Beatrice was thinking that the spell must have been dependent on Moonstone's touch, when all of a sudden, Cormac burst out from the woods. Oblivious to the raging storm, he stomped across the lawn, growling and screeching and waving his arms in fury, looking like a stunted oak gone berserk.

He marched over to where Moonstone was still attempting to wrestle Grubbs to the ground and stared at the broken limbs scattered about. Then, with lightning flashing all around him, the man-in-the-oak raised his gnarly arms to the sky and brought them down like two swift blades. The next thing Beatrice knew, Januarius Moonstone and Rollo Grubbs were buried up to their necks in the earth, their chins resting on the dead grass.

Beatrice's jaw dropped in astonishment. The heads sticking out of the turf looked like two very peculiar bowling balls. But Cormac's spell had made it impossible for the men to move, so Beatrice quickly recited her counterspell and the storm ended abruptly.

Cayenne approached the heads and sniffed at them. Then she hissed and backed away.

"My feelings exactly," Beatrice said as she turned around to speak to Cormac.

But the man-in-the-oak was gone.

About that time, Beatrice saw Mrs. Harridan and Toogood Mars coming down from the house, lanterns swinging as they hurried across the rough lawn, with the four teachers on their heels.

"I might have known!" Mrs. Harridan screeched, shooting Beatrice a furious look. "Nothing but trouble—the whole bunch of you!"

Then the woman caught sight of the stony face of Januarius Moonstone, and the weeping one of Rollo Grubbs—both of them directly at her feet—and her mouth flew open like she was preparing to scream. But gaining control of herself at the last moment, she let out a faint squeak instead.

"What—what is the meaning of this?" Mrs. Harridan stammered, holding her hand to her heart as if she expected to keel over any second. "This is the final straw! Dr. Cadwallader, you have no choice but to send these students back where they belong. All the bad habits they've learned from mortals can't be undone. Surely you must agree with me after this!"

Dr. Cadwallader walked over to them, appearing fully recovered, although his eyes were still a little glassy.

"I've never seen anything like it," Mrs. Harridan went on. "*Never!* In all my years of working with children—"

"Nedda," Dr. Cadwallader said quietly, "will you please shut up?"

And Mrs. Harridan did, appearing thoroughly shocked.

Then the headmaster turned to Beatrice and her friends. He looked exhausted. And defeated.

"They told me you went into the caverns beneath the city," he said in a weary voice.

There was a gasp from the small knot of teachers and staff.

"And they said you discovered that there is no monster," Dr. Cadwallader added.

More gasps.

"I didn't know," the headmaster said.

"We didn't think you did," Beatrice replied.

"But you sent Milo Weir and Sadie Arrowsmith to their deaths," Kick said angrily. "You can't deny that."

"I *thought* I was sending them on a mission of great scientific importance," Dr. Cadwallader answered, his voice shaking with emotion. "I believed that what we were doing here would make the world better—if only someone would listen to me."

"But you did send them into the caverns," Kick persisted.

The headmaster nodded. "I did. But they didn't go to their deaths." He dropped his eyes to the ground. "Did they, Januarius?"

Mr. Moonstone just grunted and scowled.

"Then where are they?" Ollie asked.

"They're working in one of Januarius's factories," Dr. Cadwallader said, "making Moonstone robes and Moonstone cloaks." He raised his face to the dark sky and shuddered. "To think that all I've worked for could come to such a miserable end."

Totally confused, Beatrice said, "Wait a minute. What do you mean, they're working in his factories? What's this all about?"

"My dear friend, Januarius Moonstone," Dr. Cadwallader said with a look of distaste, "needed more money than he was making with his clothing line. Why don't you tell them, Januarius? You expressed yourself so well back in my office, but I didn't catch all the details."

Mr. Moonstone's scowl deepened, but he said nothing.

"I'll tell them," Rollo Grubbs burst out, sniffling as the tears continued to roll down his face. Cutting his eyes at Moonstone, he said, "Apparently, it costs an arm and a leg to comb the Earth looking for rare animals— and not just rare, but those descended from creatures immortalized in myth. So Januarius needed to find a way to expand his factories and get free labor to work in

216

them. That's how he came up with the idea of the monster—a brilliant cover, really, so that no one would ever wonder why witches kept disappearing. Then he placed an enchantment over the city so that the panicked residents couldn't leave and deprive him of future workers."

"But Januarius couldn't pull it off on his own," Dr. Cadwallader said, looking at the mayor with contempt, "so he approached Rollo here, and offered to cut him in. And they've both been living happily—and richly—ever after for the past eleven years."

That was when Januarius Moonstone suddenly roared, "It wasn't for me! It was for the animals! Everything was for those glorious, magical creatures that *no one* appreciates the way I do. It was a noble cause!"

"A noble cause?" Dr. Cadwallader's voice was filled with disgust. "You aren't trying to *protect* those animals. You collect them like trophies. They just aren't on your walls. Admit it, owning creatures descended from the animals of the gods makes *you* feel godlike. If you'd been doing something truly noble, you wouldn't have had to hide it from me."

"Oh, don't get righteous with me," Mr. Moonstone snarled. "Rollo and I discussed telling you about it and giving you a share—thinking you might send a steady stream of students into the caverns—but we realized you were too obsessed with your stupid theory to care about money. You would have just messed everything up—as you have, tonight."

"So why bother to tell me now?" the headmaster asked listlessly. "Why didn't you just kill me as soon as you knew what these kids had found out?"

"That's what he planned to do once he got you to his house," Rollo Grubbs said, weeping in earnest now. "And then he was going to come back for the kids. But *I* didn't want you dead, Hodge! You're my friend."

"Oh, put a lid on it," Moonstone snapped. "As if friendship means anything to you. And *you*," he stormed at Cadwallader. "Don't even pretend that it was principles that made you threaten to report us tonight. You panicked—afraid that what we were doing would jeopardize that nonexistent reputation of yours as a brilliant and original mind. And don't try to tell me that you cared for one second what happened to your students."

Dr. Cadwallader stared hard at the man before he said, "I won't."

The deadness in his voice made Beatrice shiver as her eyes fell on Mrs. Harridan, then on Dr. Puffin and the others. She saw the shock and disbelief on their faces, and was relieved. It seemed clear that the teachers and staff—for all their faults—hadn't known about Cadwallader sending students into the tunnels.

"It was you who sent those men to kidnap me off the bus," Beatrice said, looking back at Moonstone. "But why?"

The man just curled his lip into a sneer, but Rollo Grubbs said eagerly, "Considering everything we'd read about you, he thought you might start nosing around—which you have—and discover the truth. So he decided to send you to one of his factories. And if that didn't work, he'd scare you off—or make Widdershins seem so awful, you'd *want* to leave. It really didn't matter, as long as you were out of the way."

"The hexes," Teddy muttered, "and the maggots in her cereal."

"The frothy-mouth dragon," Ollie added, staring coldly at Moonstone. "But it's all over now, so why don't you lift the enchantment?"

The man shot Ollie a venomous look.

"You might as well," Dr. Cadwallader said. "The authorities should go easier on you if you cooperate. I'm getting ready to call them."

"Now, Hodge," Mr. Moonstone said, his tone suddenly taking on an unconvincing friendliness, "there's no need for that. I've got enough money to set us up someplace where they'll never find us. And you know they'll lock you up, too. You've endangered the lives of your students."

Dr. Cadwallader shrugged. "So what? Once this gets out, I'll never be taken seriously as a scholar—and that's all I've ever wanted. Januarius, you have this one chance to help yourself. Lift the enchantment."

"I can't without the use of my arms," Mr. Moonstone said in a whining voice. "Dig me out of here and I'll do it."

"You don't need your arms to break an enchantment," Dr. Cadwallader said, "just your mouth."

The silence stretched out, with Beatrice and her friends waiting anxiously to see what would happen next. Finally, glaring at the headmaster, Januarius

219

Moonstone began to mumble something under his breath.

When he was finished, Dr. Cadwallader nodded and then turned to his assistant. "Toogood, would you be so kind as to complete one final assignment for me?"

"Yes, sir," Toogood Mars answered in a strangled voice, looking like he might start crying.

The headmaster touched Cyrus on the arm and said, "Escort this young witch to the Moonstone property line and see if he can step over it."

"Yes, sir," Toogood said again, wiping at his nose with a handkerchief.

Cyrus left with the man, and when they returned a few minutes later, Beatrice could tell from the grin on Cyrus's face that he was free.

She turned toward the trees and said softly, "Thank you, Cormac."

23

The End . . . and the Beginning

After three hours sleep, Beatrice woke up feeling surprisingly well and wide awake. The worries about Cyrus and the monster—not to mention, fieldwork that might have left them all dead—had been lifted, and she felt like celebrating.

She looked out the window and saw that it was snowing. The campus had been transformed from a gray and somber place where nasty secrets lurked to a landscape so beautiful it didn't seem quite real. But it was real enough to make Beatrice run to the closet for her boots and mittens.

Ten minutes later, Teddy and Iris were knocking on her door.

"I missed it *all!*" Iris wailed.

"You told her?" Beatrice asked Teddy.

"Every bizarre detail."

"And I missed it all," Iris repeated mournfully.

"Well," Beatrice said, "there were parts you should be *glad* you missed." She held out her arms and Cayenne jumped into them. "Come on, brave girl, let's go have breakfast. Iris, did Teddy tell you about Cayenne saving my life?"

When they reached the second-floor landing, they saw that the front hall was packed with students, teachers, and staff. *What's happened now?* Beatrice wondered.

As it turned out, Dr. Puffin had called an impromptu meeting before they went in to breakfast. Ollie waved to the girls and they squeezed through the crowd to join him and Cyrus and Kick. Meanwhile, Dr. Puffin had gone to stand on the stairs and was gazing out over the faces turned expectantly toward her. That untamed hair of hers was as startling as ever, and she seemed to have added a couple of extra layers to her ragtag ensemble, but beneath all the disarray was a calm sturdiness that Beatrice found reassuring.

"Good morning, students," Dr. Puffin said. "I know you were awakened by the noise and vibrations last night, and that—*unlikely* thunderstorm. I just want to tell you briefly what I know before too many false rumors get started. First of all, there is no monster living under Arcana and there never has been."

This announcement was met with exclamations of surprise and excited whispers.

"Secondly," Dr. Puffin went on, "the enchantment over the city has been lifted and its residents can leave any time they wish." Then, with a trace of sadness, she said, "And lastly, I'm sorry to have to tell you that Dr. Cadwallader has left Widdershins and isn't expected to return."

There were fewer whispers this time. But then Beatrice imagined that every student in the academy had been looking out a window when the witch police had pulled up in the wee hours of the morning to take the headmaster and his two friends away.

A few students did call out questions—*Why was Dr. Cadwallader arrested? Is it true that he and Grubbs and Moonstone were selling illegal potions?*—but Dr. Puffin held up a hand to quiet them and said, "I'll be meeting with you later in the week, once we have more details, and I'll try to answer all your questions honestly. You see, in Dr. Cadwallader's absence, the Department of Witch Education has made me acting headmistress of Widdershins."

There was applause, some polite, some genuinely enthusiastic. Beatrice was in the latter group. She hadn't gotten to know Dr. Puffin very well, but she was pretty sure the woman wouldn't be sending students off to be swallowed up by monsters. And that would be a definite improvement.

"I hope all of you will remain here," Dr. Puffin continued, "and help build Widdershins into the truly fine academy I know it can be. But if you wish to leave, the department has asked me to tell you that you'll be allowed to transfer to another school."

When she heard that, Teddy released an astonished breath and then her face broke into a grin.

"I want you to know that the curriculum at Widdershins will be expanded," Dr. Puffin told them, "to include many aspects of witch psychology, not just magical intuition. The faculty and I will be meeting this week to work that out. And now, as my first official act as headmistress," she said, actually giving them a hint of a smile, "I'm declaring this a school holiday. Go outside and play in the snow or curl up with a good book. The only thing off limits today is studying."

This brought heartfelt applause and even cheers from the students. Looking around at all the happy faces, and listening to the excited babble of voices, it seemed to Beatrice that Widdershins had finally come alive.

On their way into the dining room, Dr. Puffin came over to Beatrice and her friends. "The authorities will want to speak to you again in the next day or two," she said, "to take your official statements. In the meantime, I want to tell you how very proud I am of all of you. You're smart and brave, and what you've done for the people of this city—for all of us!—is really quite remarkable. You're just the kind of students Widdershins needs."

They were all beaming at her, pleased and a little embarrassed—except for Teddy, who didn't embarrass easily and was too ecstatic to feel anything other than joy, and Kick, who obviously had something on his mind.

"Dr. Puffin," he said, "what about all the people who were taken to Moonstone's factories? Have you heard anything about them?"

"They've been released, poor souls." The teacher spoke softly, but her eyes flashed with anger. "Mr. Moonstone," she added, grimacing as she said the name, "had them under a spell to keep them from escaping, but the doctors believe it's self-limiting and should wear off soon. Meanwhile, they've been taken to hospitals around the Sphere to be cared for."

"Were Milo and Sadie found?" he asked.

"They were," Dr. Puffin said, her expression decidedly brighter, "and they're both fine. Their parents are en route to the hospital now."

"You saved your friend," Beatrice said to Kick.

"Not alone, I didn't. Thank goodness you guys came to Widdershins. If I'd gone down in that tunnel by myself, I might be making Moonstone robes right now."

All of us would be, Beatrice thought, *if it weren't for the fox.*

She turned back to Dr. Puffin. "What about the animals in the wildlife preserve? What's going to happen to them?"

"Witches from animal welfare have stepped in," Dr. Puffin answered. "They're contacting the various areas where the animals came from and arranging to send them back home. From what they've learned, it seems that Mr. Moonstone *stole* some of them." She shook her head, causing two wiry strands of hair to pop up like antennae. "Those animals weren't neglected or abused. He *kidnapped* them!"

After their new headmistress had left, Beatrice and her friends were heading for a table when Diantha came sidling over. Of course, she acted as if no one but Ollie was there.

"I've been hearing that you're a hero," Diantha said, giving Ollie the biggest, phoniest smile Beatrice had ever seen. "Come sit with my friends and me and tell us all about it."

His face flooding with color, Ollie said, "I'm afraid you've been misinformed, Diantha. I'm *no* hero, so I have nothing to tell. Besides, I don't want to leave *my* friends."

Diantha looked surprised. Then her eyes narrowed and she dropped the pretense of being pleasant. "Your loss," she snapped. "I thought you were different, but I see now that you're just like everyone else in this loser school. I can't wait to go to a *real* academy."

To Beatrice's relief, Diantha flounced off without another word. But then she noticed that Ollie was looking downright gloomy, and it flashed through her mind that he might actually *care* what Diantha thought.

Teddy was watching Ollie, too. "What's the matter with you?" she asked bluntly.

Ollie sighed. "I used her," he said. "I was nice to her just to get information."

"So you're feeling guilty?" Teddy asked. "Well, get over it. Diantha Winter-Rose uses *everybody*. She used Milo, and she was using you, too, Ollie—just because you're cute."

Ollie turned pink again and everyone laughed.

"So are you guys going to stay at Widdershins?" Iris asked.

"No way!" Teddy said emphatically. "With any luck, I'll be at Honoria Wagstaffe before the weekend."

"I'll finish out the year, like I planned," Kick said. "Then it's back to the mortal world for me. What about you, Iris?"

"I think I want to transfer to an academy that focuses on healing," Iris said. Then she smiled sheepishly. "And one that doesn't have a resident monster—fake or otherwise."

"And, Ollie," Teddy said, "you and Beatrice can transfer to that brain school now."

"Yes," Ollie said thoughtfully, "we could, I guess."

Teddy looked from Ollie to Beatrice and back again. "But you aren't going to," she said, as if she'd just realized a horrible truth. "You're both staying here, aren't you? Are you *insane?*"

"Well, I'd still like to see if I have magical intuition," Ollie said. "Besides, things should be different with Dr. Puffin in charge."

"And I like the idea of studying witch psychology," Beatrice added. "Who knows? That might turn out to be my field."

"Oh, puh-*lease,*" Teddy said, rolling her eyes. "You two *need* witch psychology. I'd say ten or fifteen years of intensive therapy might do it."

Beatrice just shrugged and grinned. She really was going to miss Teddy. Then she turned to Cyrus. "So what are *you* going to do, Cyrus?"

"I might be back," he said, "but right now, I just want to go home. I need to talk to my parents about—well, all that's happened."

Beatrice nodded. "Just don't forget," she said, "they love you to distraction."

Cyrus smiled. "I never doubted that for a minute."

"I haven't heard from Miranda yet," she told him.

"It doesn't matter," Cyrus replied. "Silva and Ogden Rascallion are my parents, no matter what the adoption records say."

Then Teddy said, "Cyrus, I was wondering if you'd given any thought to talking to Januarius Moonstone. I mean, just in case he turns out to be . . . you know."

"I have nothing to say to him," Cyrus said firmly. "He's a terrible man—and wherever his son is, I think he's lucky he got away. I've been going over all this in my mind, and I've decided that Liliana knew what her husband was up to and didn't want her son growing up with a father like that. I mean, she asked Zipporah to take her child to safety just hours before the monster appeared for the first time. Coincidence? I don't think so."

"Neither do I," Ollie said. "I think you've figured it out."

"And even though Moonstone didn't actually kill Liliana," Cyrus continued, "he's the one who came up with that phony monster—so he's still responsible for her death. At least, that's how I see it."

Everyone murmured their agreement.

"Beatrice, I've just decided," Cyrus added. "If Miranda does find those adoption records, I don't want to know. Maybe someday, but not now."

Beatrice nodded and said gently, "It's your choice, Cyrus."

"There's only one thing I wish," he said softly.

"What's that?" Beatrice asked.

"That I could talk to Liliana for just a few minutes," he said. "To thank her. For myself, if I am her son. And, if not, for another thirteen-year-old boy out there."

They spent most of the day outside, having snow-ball fights and building a large snow cat, complete with broom-straw whiskers and Teddy's knit cap. Cayenne leaped up on the snow cat's head, settled into the fuzzy wool, and drifted off to sleep.

Cyrus played outside for a while, then went to the kitchen for a long talk with Zipporah. Later, he came back with a treat for everyone—Zipporah's roasted apples sprinkled with fairy dust.

It was nearly time for dinner when Beatrice went upstairs to change clothes and towel Cayenne dry. Before meeting her friends, she checked her quick-mail, and there was a message from Miranda. Her eyes darting down the screen, Beatrice read the words eagerly.

Hi, Cuz! Hope things have improved since your last quick-mail. I won't bore you with the details, but getting into the Institute's adoption records proved impossible. You have no idea how snotty civil servants can be. So I talked to Dr. Featherstone, who got the record you needed in about two minutes.

Beatrice's heart was beating fast as she read the next paragraph.

*A two-year-old child named Finn Spitz, son of
Zipporah Spitz, was adopted approximately
eleven years ago by Silva and Ogden Rascallion.*

Miranda went on to say that she was worried about them, as was Dr. Featherstone, who planned to come to Widdershins in the next day or two to check up on them. But Beatrice stopped reading at that point because something outside had caught her eye. Holding Cayenne in her arms, she walked to the window for a closer look.

Cyrus was perched on a big rock at the edge of the woods. And sitting beside him, her copper coat glowing against the snow, was the fox spirit. Beatrice could see Cyrus's lips moving and the fox seeming to listen attentively. Then he stopped talking and they sat there quietly, the falling snow soon turning his blue cap white.

Finally, the fox stood up, and after looking into Cyrus's face for a moment, stepped into the trees. She glanced back once, as if reluctant to leave, and he raised his hand to wave. Then the animal disappeared into the woods.

Beatrice was sorry to see the fox go, but she was pretty sure that Cyrus had gotten his one wish: a chance to thank Liliana. And besides, everyone knew the fox spirit was a wanderer at heart, and only stayed as long as she was needed.